That is the true season of love, when we believe that we alone can love, that no one could ever have loved so before us, and that no one will love in the same way after us.

—GOETHE

"What Overpowering Passion You Have Hidden Within You, Cassie!"

Steele whispered huskily, his gray gaze burning into her, setting her even more aflame. "And to know it can be released at my touch . . ." His words trailed off as his lips lit a painfully sweet fire within her trembling body.

She was a beautiful creature, an enchanting woman, and Steele longed to answer the unspoken question in her tawny gold eyes. But what was she asking? What mystery lurked deep within that passion-glazed look?

SHERRY DEE

started writing as a result of a dream. She woke up and couldn't remember how it concluded, so she simply wrote her own ending. In regard to her writing, Ms. Dee admits that she has become "intrigued with the idea of making life what I want it to be . . . at least for a little while. Writing has become an important part of my life. It's as natural as breathing and I'm not ready to stop doing either."

Dear Reader:

SILHOUETTE DESIRE is an exciting new line of contemporary romances from Silhouette Books. During the past year, many Silhouette readers have written in telling us what other types of stories they'd like to read from Silhouette, and we've kept these comments and suggestions in mind in developing SILHOUETTE DESIRE.

DESIREs feature all of the elements you like to see in a romance, plus a more sensual, provocative story. So if you want to experience all the excitement, passion and joy of falling in love, then SILHOUETTE DESIRE is for you.

I hope you enjoy this book and all the wonderful stories to come from SILHOUETTE DESIRE. I'd appreciate any thoughts you'd like to share with us on new SILHOUETTE DESIRE, and I invite you to write to us at the address below:

Karen Solem
Editor-in-Chief
Silhouette Books
P.O. Box 769
New York, N.Y. 10019

SHERRY DEE
Make No Promises

Silhouette Desire

Published by Silhouette Books New York

America's Publisher of Contemporary Romance

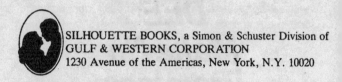

SILHOUETTE BOOKS, a Simon & Schuster Division of GULF & WESTERN CORPORATION
1230 Avenue of the Americas, New York, N.Y. 10020

ISBN: 0–671–44900–1

First Silhouette Books printing July, 1982

10 9 8 7 6 5 4 3 2 1

America's Publisher of Contemporary Romance

Printed in the U.S.A.

Acknowledgments

Denise Marcil, *who was a great source of strength and encouragement. She never restricted my sensitivity or creativity; she only showed me the way to be better. Denise is more than an agent—she's a friend.*

Karen Solem, *for her interest and belief in my work. Through her I have learned that patience does not mean indifference, and positiveness helps one to grow.*

1

~~~~~~~~~

Cassie Layton hurriedly made her way along the wide, red-carpeted corridor toward the large glass double doors of the main casino.

She was late and Paul would be furious with her, she was thinking. Paul had said, "Seven o'clock, Cass, and not a minute past! This is a big night for me, I can feel it!" Cassie had assured him that seven o'clock it would be.

But the bellboy had been late bringing her clothes from the hotel cleaners and it had caused Cassie an unexpected delay.

Well, it didn't matter now, the girl thought wearily, and with a deep sigh she glanced at the small gold watch on her arm which showed the time to be fifteen minutes past the hour of seven. There was nothing to be done about it, Cassie reasoned, so Paul would be in a foul mood as he always was when things didn't go his way.

Pushing open the heavy door, Cassie stepped into the

hazy, smoke-filled room. The roar of voices rang above the hum of spinning roulette wheels. She heard the clear sound of silver as it splashed from the mouths of the one-armed bandits and listened to the voices, both male and female, swearing, laughing, shouting out their victories as well as their defeats.

Cassie's warm brown eyes carefully examined her surroundings, searching the crowded room for Paul, then rested upon his tall slim figure seated at a blackjack table, a large stack of red chips at his elbow.

Paul Malone was a nice-looking man, not what one would call "handsome," but his beachboy good looks, dark blue eyes, and sandy brown hair had won the heart of Cassie Layton.

As Cassie moved to the table and stood behind him, Paul glanced up at her with a look of irritation on his face. She smiled and murmured, "Sorry I'm so late," but Paul merely frowned and returned his full attention to the game.

The dealer gave each player a card, face down, then dealt one for himself before dealing out a second card, face up, to each. Cassie watched with interest as each player peeped at the face-down card which had been dealt him.

"Card?" asked the dealer. The little gray-haired lady at Cassie's right shook her head and the dealer moved on to Paul.

"Hit me!" Paul tapped his cards and spoke without glancing up.

The dealer added a jack to Paul's two-of-clubs. Cassie's heart sank as Paul's hand flattened angrily on his cards and he choked, "Busted!" Turning his remaining face-down card over to reveal a king, Paul pushed himself abruptly from the table and strode away.

Quickening her steps, Cassie hurried to catch up with

Paul's long, angry strides as he headed toward the bar and ordered a scotch and water.

"How much did you lose?" she asked in concern.

"Enough!" was Paul's curt reply. "Why weren't you here at seven as I told you to be? You know I can't concentrate when I don't know where you are!" Before Cassie could answer, Paul immediately demanded, "Hand over a hundred!" As she made no move to do so, he rasped out, "You did bring some money with you, didn't you?"

"Uh—yes! Yes, you told me to bring money, so I did," Cassie stammered.

"All right, then hand it over!"

"A hundred, Paul? All I have left is three hundred. Can't you use some of the money you won last night?" Cassie pleaded.

"I don't have it!" Paul gulped the last of his drink. "I left it in my hotel room," he amended.

Cassie watched his face as he spoke. He hadn't left the money in his room, she thought in apprehension, he had gambled it away. Why was it that Paul felt he must always lie to her? Why couldn't he just admit that he had gambled and lost?

"Come on, Cass, if I can win a bundle we can go on with our plans," Paul wheedled, his hands stroking her honey-colored hair. "We can't get married if we don't have enough money to start a life together."

"But, Paul! You told me to sell my car and my jewelry and that the proceeds, added to what you already had, would be enough money. And now . . ." Cassie's words trailed off as her voice broke.

"Are you saying you're sorry you did so? Are you telling me you're sorry you came with me?"

"Oh, Paul, that isn't it at all!" Cassie wrung her hands nervously, trying to find the right words. "Nassau is beautiful! I've never seen a place so lovely! But we—that is—well, you said we would be married when we got here, that this would be our honeymoon. Paul, you promised, and we've been here for three weeks already. And still we aren't married! All you've done since we've been here is to gamble away almost all the money!"

"My God, Cass! Are you going to start that again?" Paul ground out the words as his empty glass crashed down on the teakwood bar. "I can't stand a whining female, nor, might I add, a clinging vine. I won't have it, Cass!"

Cassie checked the tears which had sprung unbidden to her brown eyes. She was fully aware that Paul's words had been heard by the bartender as well as others around them. She felt the curious stares and glanced self-consciously about, her sherry-brown eyes momentarily meeting the clear gray eyes of a tall, handsome stranger who lounged near the entrance.

The compassion which shone in the depths of those gray eyes let Cassie know that Paul's words had carried to the ears of that stranger and she lowered her head in embarrassment.

"I—I'm sorry, Paul," she whispered contritely, "I didn't mean to sound as if I were whining. I—I . . . well . . . oh, never mind!"

And with that Cassie turned and fled from the room, the tears spilling over.

Long, tanned fingers toyed absently at the corners of the worn photograph of a beautiful young woman. Smoky-gray eyes studied the striking beauty of the image which looked back with sherry-brown eyes shot with gold. The honey-brown hair was windblown, causing sun-kissed, featherlike tresses to frame the lightly tanned oval face.

How many times in the three weeks just past had he

retrieved the photo from his breast pocket to look at the lovely face, Steele Malone wondered. How often had this young beauty haunted him?

Running a thumb along the jawline of the girl in the snapshot, Steele imagined that he could feel her smooth, silken skin. His thumb moved on to outline the sensual, pouty lips.

There was an innocent look about her that made it difficult for Malone to believe that this girl was his brother's mistress. But the facts were all there. Steele sighed deeply as he placed the photo back in his pocket.

Malone had hired Fred Hall, a private investigator, to check on Steele's younger brother, Paul, and to report Paul's whereabouts, with whom he associated, how much money he was spending, and how it was spent. Hall was to hold back nothing!

Then, three weeks ago, Hall had come to Steele's office and handed Steele the snapshot.

"Her name's Cassandra Layton—'Cassie' to her *friends.*" Hall's words carried a double meaning. "She's twenty-one years old, five feet three and, I'd say, about one-hundred-five pounds."

Opening his brown leather note pad, the investigator began to read aloud.

"No family. She worked as a typist—" an amused chuckle preceded his next words, "—a 'girl Friday,' so to speak, at Rodale's. Worked there close to a year. Then she met your brother about two months back and they've been dating ever since. And two days ago Miss Layton quit her job, sold her belongings, and the two of 'em flew to the Bahamas. They're there now!"

Fred Hall concluded his verbal report by giving Steele the name of a well-known hotel where he could find his brother and Cassie Layton.

Now, three weeks later, Steele Malone was in Nassau having just finished the annual Miami-Nassau ocean race in which he had come in with a tie for third place. Steele was an avid sailor and his love for the ocean and the out-of-doors kept his free time filled. He had been excited about the race and felt that he would have done better had he not missed the last two races due to the pressures of his business.

Following the race, Steele had anchored his sleek, forty-five-foot yawl, showered and shaved, then changed into appropriate clothing for a night in the casino. Going ashore, Malone hailed a taxi and gave the driver the address of his favorite night spot.

As the cab stopped before the club, Steele unfolded his lithe frame from the taxi, paid the driver and approached the door of the casino. He stopped in mid-stride as he saw a lovely young woman hurriedly enter the door ahead of him. It was Cassandra Layton, the girl in the photograph which he had carried with him for days.

Quickly Steele followed the girl and watched as Cassie hurried across the lobby and down the corridor toward the casino. He saw her pause outside the heavy door and glance at her watch before pushing open the door and stepping into the room.

Not far behind Cassie, Steele reached the door just seconds later and he, too, entered the gaming room. He sauntered over to a nearby slot machine and casually leaned against it where he could observe the goings-on.

Steele's cool gray eyes followed as Cassie headed purposefully to a blackjack table. He had to admit that Cassandra Layton was even more beautiful in the flesh. Too beautiful! His eyes took in the graceful swing of her shapely hips, every curve of her attractive body which was detailed in the clinging halter jumpsuit of peach-colored silk.

When Cassie reached her destination, Steele's gaze rested upon his wayward younger brother, Paul Malone. For a few minutes Steele stood watching the tableau before him. He could not hear the brief words of the girl, but he noted the irritation on his brother's face as he looked up at her and returned to his game. Paul's angry actions indicated to Steele that he had lost.

His eyes followed the pair as Cassie hurried to match Paul's long strides toward the bar. He could not help but see the grave concern on the girl's lovely face. A few moments passed in which Steele could tell that their conversation was rapidly becoming a quarrel. Then he heard his brother's voice rise angrily. "I won't have it, Cass!"

At Paul's rude outburst, Steele felt a stab of compassion for the lovely Cassie as she glanced about her at those who must certainly have heard. For a moment her warm brown eyes met his and Steele could not fail to see the hurt in them before she lowered her head and fled from the room. Steele stiffened in disgust at the cunning smile on his brother's face as he ordered another drink and turned with interest to the buxom blonde who had taken the stool beside him.

Cassie was in tears when she reached her room. She threw open the door, then slammed it behind her, and flung herself across the bed. Why had Paul done this to her, she wondered, why had he embarrassed her so? There seemed to be so much about him that she did not understand. She dissolved into tears and cried until she fell into an exhausted sleep.

Sometime later Cassie was awakened by a determined knock on the door. She stirred and sat up, whisking the soft brown hair from her face.

"Cassie? Open the door, babe," came Paul's hushed voice from the other side of the wooden barrier. "Cassie?"

"Go away, Paul!" Cassie called out. "Please, just go away."

"Ah, come on, Cass. Open the door, will you. I wanta talk to you." Paul sounded hurt and soft-hearted Cassie crossed the room to open the door.

"Sorry about the fight, Cass," were Paul's first words. "But sometimes you have a way of rubbing a guy the wrong way." He sat down on the bed, but Cassie remained standing just inside the closed door. "I have a surprise for you and I guess I'll have to tell you about it so that you'll understand." Patting the side of the bed where he sat, Paul coaxed, "Come, sit by me while I tell you."

Willing to bridge the gap that the quarrel had caused, Cassie obediently walked over to Paul and sat by him.

"Paul, I—" Cassie began.

"Forget it!" Paul broke in, not wanting to hear what he was sure she was about to say, nearly certain that it would be about the money he had squandered.

"But I—" she tried again.

"Cass, I said I have a surprise! Don't you want to know what it is?" Paul asked with his boyish grin.

"Sure, Paul, what is the surprise?" Cassie asked halfheartedly.

"The money that I've won, Cass, was used for a good cause. I haven't gambled it all away, as you have accused. You see, Cass, I've bought a boat!"

"A boat? But, Paul! Why on earth—"

"She's a beaut, Cass! You'll love her!" Paul's enthusiasm seemed genuine. "She's a forty-five footer, a dream on the water, and she cost a bundle but it was worth it! I've named her *Malone's Passion,* but I bought her for you, Cass!" He paused to look closely at Cassie, as if to determine whether or not he was convincing her. Paul watched the play of emotions on Cassie's face and wondered what she was thinking.

When Cassie made no comment, Paul continued. "We can live on the boat, Cass, and we won't need an

apartment. We can dock her in Miami and live on her."
Paul took Cassie's hands in both of his and lifted them to
his lips. "Well, I thought you'd be happy, babe." He
managed a disappointed sigh, then stood and began to
pace the room. "Okay, Cass, so I made a bad move,
buying a sloop without first talking it over with you,
finding out if you'd like it. So I'll sell her."

Paul had smoothly turned the tables on her, causing
her to feel that she had mistreated him, that he was the
injured party and she was to blame. To Cassie, Paul
looked like a little boy who had brought home a puppy,
only to be told that he couldn't keep it.

"Oh, no, Paul!" Cassie breathed. "You mustn't sell
her! I couldn't let you do that! I was just taken off guard,
that's all." She raised her hand and let it slide around
Paul's neck and assured him, "I'm happy about your
choice, really I am. I've never lived on a boat but I'm sure
I'll be happy wherever you are. And if you want to live
aboard a yawl, or boat, or whatever you call it, then that's
what we'll do!"

"Are you sure, Cass? I want you to be happy," Paul
said, gathering her into his arms.

"Of course, I'm sure!" Cassie hoped her voice
wouldn't give away her true feelings. She would do what
she must to make Paul happy and if it meant living on a
boat, then that's what she would do!

"Good! We'll leave in the morning for Miami!" Paul
told Cassie as he put her away from him and stared into
her big brown eyes. "That is, if you can have your things
packed and ready to put aboard first thing in the
morning."

"I'll be ready, Paul," Cassie said bravely.

"Fine! I'll see you in the morning," Paul told her,
starting for the door. Suddenly he stopped and wheeled
about. "Oh, I almost forgot, Cass. I need the rest of our

money so I can stock the boat with provisions and hire a boy to help sail her back to Miami.''

Cassie suppressed a sigh as she walked to the dresser where her purse lay. With her back turned to Paul, she withdrew the last three hundred dollars of her money. Before turning back, she furtively tucked a few bills into the bottom of her bag and covered them with the other articles within. Crossing over to Paul, Cassie held her breath, hoping he would not count the money since she had told him earlier how much she had.

Paul was speaking but she had missed part of what he said. "—all right?"

"W—what? I'm sorry, Paul, I didn't hear you," Cassie stammered, watching Paul stuff the money into his wallet and replace it in his coat pocket.

"I said, we'll get married when we get back to Miami, all right? Wait!" Paul held up his hand to silence Cassie when he saw that she was about to speak. "We'll get married, I'll take a one-month leave of absence, draw some money out of savings, and we'll sail at random for our honeymoon. How does that sound?"

Cassie threw her arms about his neck. "Oh, Paul, it sounds heavenly! Do you mean it, really mean it?"

"Sure, babe, that's what I've planned all along. But it's all arranged, now," Paul concluded as he opened the door. "You get to bed, now, we have to get up early." Placing a light kiss on Cassie's lips, Paul left the room.

Cassie was elated. After all the waiting, all her uncertainties, she was finally to become Paul's wife! He hadn't lied to her as she had thought! She went into the bathroom, washed the tears from her cheeks and brushed her silky honey-colored hair. She was happy, really happy, and she realized that she was humming as she faced the starry-eyed girl in the mirror.

Then Cassie remembered that she must start packing,

and as she removed her luggage from the closet she realized that Paul had not said what time she was to be ready to leave. He had just said "early."

She went to the telephone and asked the hotel operator to connect her to Paul's room. She listened to the ringing of the phone, waiting excitedly for Paul's airy "Hello." After a time, the operator came back on the line to say that there was no answer and asked if she could take a message. Cassie thanked her, replied that there was no message, and thoughtfully replaced the receiver.

Cassie sat heavily on the bed, bewildered that Paul hadn't answered his phone. Had he gone back out? If so, where could he be? Then she decided that he must be in the shower and drew a relieved breath. Well, she'd give him time to finish his bath, then she would try again.

Leaving Cassie's room, Paul walked down the hall to the elevator and pushed the "Down" button. When the elevator doors did not open immediately, he muttered a curse and waited impatiently until the car reached his floor. Stepping in, he pushed the button marked "Lobby" and leaned casually against the padded wall, watching the numbers wink on and off as they passed the various floors. As the elevator doors slid open, Paul made his way to the hotel desk, tossed his key to the night clerk, and took his bag from a waiting bellboy. He handed the boy a silver dollar and strode to the outer door where a cab waited. Opening the door of the taxi, Paul climbed into the back seat giving the driver a one-word order, "Airport!"

Steele Malone had entered the hotel lobby just as his brother, Paul, left the elevator. Pressing his large frame behind a tall potted palm, Steele eyed the scene before him, and when Paul passed through the large double

19

doors on his way to the cab, Steele could easily have
reached out and touched him. Then the voice of his
brother clearly reached Steele's ears as he gave his
destination to the driver.

Airport? Then his little argument with Cassie must
have resulted in a breakup, Steele surmised.

Moving away from the shadow of the large palm,
Steele walked across the lobby to a row of pay phones.
He would call Fred Hall and tell him to resume the
investigation, he decided, hoping that Paul was headed
back to Miami and that Fred wouldn't have to track him
down elsewhere.

Steele completed his telephone conversation with Hall,
then returned to the casino to try his luck. But his
thoughts were on Cassie and he wondered where she
was now. Had she already left? If so, where had she
gone? Would he ever see her again? The latter question
was the one which bothered Steele Malone the most.

"Mr. Malone has checked out, Miss," the stocky desk
clerk told Cassie.

"Checked out? But when?" she asked in surprise.

"About an hour ago," came the answer.

"Did he leave a message? Did he say where he was
going, where he could be reached?"

"No, Miss, he didn't. You might ask the bartender or
one of the bellboys. Sometimes they overhear a guest tell
a cabbie where they're going."

"You mean Mr. Malone left in a taxi?" Cassie asked,
unbelievingly.

"Matter of fact, he did, Miss. Sorry, that's all I know,"
and the clerk turned away to tuck an envelope in a mail
slot behind the desk.

"Thank you," Cassie choked as she turned away in
complete bewilderment.

She had tried repeatedly to reach Paul by phone, packing her bags in the meantime. When it became apparent that he had not returned to his room, Cassie had decided that Paul must have returned to the casino, since he had got more money from her. But he wasn't in the casino, either, so she had checked with the desk clerk as a last resort.

Why would Paul leave the hotel at this time of night, Cassie wondered, and where would he— The boat! Of course, she thought, he had gone to the boat! Chiding herself for distrusting Paul, Cassie smiled in relief and hurried back to her room to complete her packing. She would pick up her bags in the morning, she determined, but she wanted to go on to the boat tonight.

Cassie paused as she snapped the latch on her overnight case, wondering how she would find Paul's boat. He hadn't told her where it was, only that he had named her *Malone's Passion*. Oh, well, she mused, all she need do was to go down to the harbor and look for it.

Placing all her luggage in a neat row along the wall, Cassie picked up her purse and left the room. She felt confident that she would have no problem in locating a sailboat named *Malone's Passion!*

Cassie slipped quietly along the weather-beaten wharf, her bare feet soundless on the damp wood as she carefully made her way through the darkness. The night was deadly still. An eerie quiet lay over the pier and only the small sliver of a pale moon hung in the black velvet sky.

She held a deathlike grip on her shoulder bag with one hand and carried her low-heeled sandals in the other, her eyes desperately trying to focus in the darkness of the night. Her tawny-brown eyes glimmered in the pale light as they searched eagerly for Paul's boat. The names of the yawls were veiled in duskiness and Cassie had trouble reading them. The masts of sailboats, sloops, and fishing vessels reached upward toward the sky, resembling a tangled network of haunting timbers.

Suddenly Cassie halted to admire the sleek lines of a sailboat somewhat larger and more stately than its neighbors. Stepping closer, she read the name which was beautifully scripted in bold letters against a startling white coat of paint—*Malone's Passion!*

With a quick intake of breath, Cassie marveled at the beauty of the boat for a moment before starting up the ladderlike steps. Lowering herself to the deck, Cassie's shirt caught on a protruding object—she wasn't sure what—but it ripped the shirt down the front as she jerked away. Her sudden movement caused her to lose her balance, and she tripped over a tack box and crashed to the deck. One flailing hand grasped the loose corner of a tarpaulin and it followed her to the floor, partially covering her body.

Cassie stifled an insane urge to giggle. She had wanted to surprise Paul, she thought, but this was ridiculous!

Suddenly a shaft of bright light from the open doorway of the cabin silhouetted the tall figure of a man who stood above Cassie. Strong arms lifted her to her feet and she clutched at her tattered shirt in a futile effort to hide her exposed flesh. As she stood, a stabbing pain shot through Cassie's ankle and she stumbled into the arms of the stranger.

"Are you all right?" asked a deep voice.

Cassie turned her face upward to answer but the words died on her lips and she drew in her breath sharply. The man was unbelievably handsome, with dark hair which hung in thick tousled lengths that curled about his neck.

He had a beautifully curved mouth and a dimple was carved in his right cheek. Cassie stared up into deep, steel-gray eyes that were dark with concern. Carefully scrutinizing him, she became acutely aware that he was, in turn, studying her.

Conscious of her disheveled state with her torn shirt and bare feet, Cassie didn't know that to the man staring back at her, she was a most beautiful and desirable woman. With her sherry-brown eyes wide and questioning, her unruly brown hair in disarray framing an oval face, the torn shirt partially revealing full, jutting breasts that rose and fell with each breath, and pouty, rosebud lips that still trembled slightly, Cassie was easily the most beautiful woman that he had ever encountered.

Her eyes dropped under the appraisal and Cassie nervously tugged at the torn edges of her shirt as she stepped out of the arms which still encircled her. But once again the agonizing pain claimed her ankle, and with a low moan she grasped the muscular arms for support.

"You *are* hurt?" the man asked gently.

Cassie mutely nodded her head as another searing pain seized her and the tall stranger effortlessly lifted her atop a small crate. As he stood before her, he began to unbutton his checkered flannel shirt and Cassie watched his long, tanned fingers work the buttons. Even his hands were handsome, she noted.

"Who are you? And why are you here?" The questions brought Cassie back to her situation.

"I'm Cassie—Cassie Layton, and I'm looking for Paul Malone."

"Oh?" was all the man said. He pulled the tail of his shirt free from his faded jeans and, removing the shirt from his own shoulders, placed it about Cassie's. It was warm from the heat of his body and Cassie breathed in the scent of the man, the strong odor of tobacco, and a manly musk.

"So you're here to see Paul Malone?" he queried.

"Y—yes, I was to meet him here. We're supposed to leave tomorrow." Cassie looked up questioningly. "This is the right boat, isn't it? This is *Malone's Passion?*"

"That's right," the man answered casually and, leaning forward, he proceeded to button up the shirt which Cassie had struggled into. "There!" His voice sounded quite pleased. "Feel better, now?"

Cassie wordlessly nodded her head. This man who stood before her was much too handsome. Dark hair carpeted his broad chest which was only a breath away. He was tall, lean, and powerfully built and Cassie was far too aware of him as a man. Her brown eyes drank in the sight of him.

"Now, Cassie." The words brought her out of her wonderings and she flushed as if he had read her thoughts. "I'll take you below, so you can talk to Malone."

Sweeping her into his arms, he straightened and strode toward the door.

Upon reaching the cabin below, they passed down a narrow hallway and into a bedroom. Cassie's eyes quickly searched the room for Paul but there was no sign of him.

"Paul isn't here!" Cassie gasped.

"Nope," was the brief reply.

"But where is he?" Cassie persisted as she was set upon a large bed.

"Gone!"

Panic rose within Cassie. Paul was gone and she was alone with a stranger!

"But—but you said you would take me to talk to Paul!"

"No, I said I would take you to talk to Malone," he countered. "And I did!"

"But—" Cassie began.

"I'm Steele Malone," he interrupted with a lazy smile. "Paul's brother."

"You!" Cassie almost choked in her surprise. "You're Steele Malone?"

She could only gape at the man. This was Steele Malone! According to Paul's tales, Steele Malone was an overbearing, arrogant, domineering man who was a law unto himself. He was a person whom Cassie had hoped never to meet, for Paul had unwittingly planted a seed of fear and dread within her toward this unknown man.

"You're Paul's brother?" Cassie repeated in disbelief.

"That's right, the one and only Steele Malone. Are you disappointed?" he drawled lazily as he lit a cigarette and slumped into a nearby chair.

"Well, n—no, not disappointed—I guess," she blurted. "Just surprised." Cassie stared at him for a moment. "No! No, I'm not disappointed," she repeated definitely.

"Good! Now tell me, Cassie, why you came here at this hour of the night." Steele tapped his watch significantly.

"I came because—well, I was supposed to meet Paul here early in the morning. But he didn't tell me what time, he only said 'early,' and when I tried to get in touch with him he had left the hotel and the only place he could have gone was to his boat."

Steele's eyes watched her intently, and when he made no comment a nagging doubt gripped her and she asked breathlessly, "This is Paul's boat, isn't it?"

"Paul's boat?" Instantly Steele was on his feet, towering over Cassie. His dark brows were raised and his gray eyes narrowed. "My brother's boat?" Steele's short laugh portrayed both amusement and incredulity. "Who told you that this was Paul's boat?"

"Why, Paul, of course," Cassie began uncertainly. A

sea of doubts and perplexities washed over her, but she met his eyes bravely and continued, "We are to sail back to Miami where we will be married and—"

"Married!" The words shot out of Steele's mouth and Cassie jumped at the savageness in his voice.

Why, the man is angry, Cassie thought in distress. But why? she wondered.

"Yes, married," she replied in a small voice, then continued carefully, "I told you—"

"I know what you told me," Steele interrupted, "and it doesn't make sense, Miss Layton." With an exasperated sigh he dropped back into his chair, then, watching her closely, he asked, "Do you know where Paul is?"

"I thought he might be here. The night clerk at the hotel said Paul had checked out and the only place I could think he might go—"

"Was here?" Again Steele broke in. Spreading his hands in a gesture of frustration, he gave a muttered "Damn!" and leaned forward, elbows on knees, and told Cassie bluntly, "This ketch belongs to me, Miss Layton, not my younger brother!"

"I—I don't understand," she stammered. "You're telling me that *Malone's Passion* is *your* boat and not Paul's?"

"That's right. I bought this rig six years ago with hard-earned money, named her *Malone's Passion* because of the passion I have for sailing. Paul owns no part of her, nor has he ever!"

Cassie was confused. What had Paul done, she wondered, where had he gone? Steele's words rang with truth and she realized that she had been placed in a most embarrassing situation. She tried desperately to combat the rising fear that Paul had abandoned her as well as lied to her.

She attempted to rise to her feet but the pain in her ankle stopped her most effectively, and she sank back to the bed. A wan smile crossed her face as she explained weakly, "I think I must have twisted my ankle when I fell."

"Let's have a look," Steele responded as he knelt by the bed and reached for Cassie's small foot. She winced as he moved it from side to side. Because of his nearness, Cassie could study the man before her. She noted the strong features, long dark lashes, and the tiny laughter lines at the corners of his gray eyes. Acutely aware of the gentleness of the strong hands as tanned fingers probed her swollen ankle tenderly, Cassie found herself wondering what kind of man Steele Malone was and knew instinctively that he was a far different person than his brother, Paul.

Furthermore, Cassie realized that Steele Malone didn't seem at all like the lordly, domineering man that Paul had led her to believe he was.

"No broken bones," Steele announced, getting to his feet. "Looks as if you'll have a mighty sore ankle for a couple of days, though!" Gazing down at Cassie, he continued, "I'll find something to bind it with so it won't pain you so much when you walk."

She watched as Steele disappeared through the door, then sat looking about her at the masculinity of the bedroom. No ruffles on the curtains, she noticed, just plain, straight drapes. On the dresser was a half-filled ashtray, a few crumpled cigarette packs, a hairbrush and comb. A nightstand held only a clock and a partially filled bottle of Scotch along with a single glass. It was clearly a man's room, Cassie thought, her eye catching the simple gray and black terry cloth bathrobe flung over the foot of the bed.

So engrossed was she in her thoughts that she was not aware that Steele had returned until she heard his deep, rumbling voice.

"It's not much, but it's home," he said in amusement.

"Oh," Cassie gasped nervously, "I—why, I see nothing wrong with it. And, of course, it doesn't matter what I think, you know."

"And what *do* you think, Miss Layton?"

"Just that you seem to be quite comfortable with simple things—not that this boat is simple," she amended hurriedly, "but you don't seem to have the extravagant tastes that Paul has," Cassie replied quite honestly. "You're—well, sort of rugged, down-to-earth and Paul is . . ." She trailed off, not really certain of what she meant to say.

"Ah, yes, Paul! Now, let's go from there!" Steele took up her words. "You say that Paul has checked out of the hotel and you don't know where he is, am I right?" There was a prolonged silence. Steele waited for an answer. Cassie bent her head; her trembling fingers toyed with a button on the oversized shirt she wore.

Steele made no attempt to prompt her for the answer. He waited for a brief time, then knelt before her with an ace bandage. "Let's take care of that ankle," he said simply, and with swift, sure hands he began the task of binding her swollen ankle.

"Paul has deserted me!" Cassie suddenly choked. "But why? Why would he?" When Steele's only response was a slight shrug, Cassie went on. "But we were going to be married! Paul loves me—"

"*Love!* Love!" Steele's mocking laughter echoed across the small room. "He doesn't even know the meaning of the word! Because Paul loves no one but Paul Malone!" Steele's gray gaze burned into her.

"You're wrong!" Cassie shouted as she clasped her hands over her ears trying to drown out his words. Steele rose and, grasping her wrists, he shook her violently.

"Listen to me, Cassie! Hear me!"

"No! We loved each other!" Cassie's tears began to flow freely. "We were going to be married!"

28

Steele flung Cassie from him in anger and frustration. "Can't you see? Are you so naive, so inexperienced, that you can't spot a con artist when you see one? Paul would never have married you! Never!"

"He would have! You just don't want me to believe Paul's any good, that he loves me!" a furious Cassie shot back. "Why?"

In exasperation and without thinking, Steele replied, "Paul is no good! And he's not the kind of a man for a girl like you!" Steele exploded fiercely. "God, Cassie, are you blind? He's a playboy—a rake! And he won't marry you because . . . because he's already married!"

At Steele's words Cassie felt as if the earth had suddenly dropped from beneath her. Her mind seemed to scream, "I told you so! I told you so!"

Cassie found herself remembering many things that had happened in the days since she had met Paul Malone, things which, at the time, had given her a vague feeling of uncertainty and which she had shrugged off. Some of the remarks Paul had made had also caused her some uneasiness. All of this, coupled with his harshness, gambling habits, and excessive drinking seemed to cross her mind as on a moving picture screen. Suddenly she realized that although it hurt to have to admit it, Paul Malone had played her for a fool!

It had been lies! All lies! She closed her eyes tightly, trying to believe it was all a bad dream, but when she opened them, Cassie stared straight into the clear gray eyes of Steele. She knew it was not a dream, but the blunt truth.

"So, what will you do now?" Steele asked quietly.

"I'll find Paul!" Cassie stated firmly to Steele. Despite its betraying tremble, she held her small chin high and as tears still burned her eyes she continued, "I'll find him, I'll face Paul, and I'll hear all you have just told me from Paul himself, before I'll believe what you've said!"

"Little fool!" Steele hissed between clenched teeth.

Cassie lifted her head and swiping her hand angrily across her eyes to dash away the tears which threatened to fall, she met Steele's eyes bravely.

"Maybe so. But I'll live with myself when I know for sure. And with your help, Mr. Malone, I'll find Paul and come to that conclusion."

"*My* help?" he questioned in disbelief. "How can—"

"I'm going back to Miami with you, Mr. Malone," she stated bluntly.

"You're *what?*" he roared.

Cassie stared at him, apprehension tugging at her when she saw that his eyes had darkened dangerously. "I—I said I could go back to Miami with you."

"That's what I thought you said!" Shaking his head violently, Steele gave a short, mirthless laugh. "Oh, no! No, Cassie Layton, you're not going anywhere with me! Now, you get yourself up and I'll take you back to your hotel!" his voice rang out harshly. Cassie thought, how like his name he was. Steele was as hard and cold as steel. Yes, his name suited him well!

"Come on, let's get going!" But when Cassie made no move, Steele ordered roughly, "Come on! *Now!*"

"No! I—I can't!" she whispered pleadingly. "I checked out of the hotel. I have no place to go!"

"Oh, for God's sake," Steele began exasperatedly. "Try another excuse!"

"But it *isn't* just an excuse! Oh, Steele, please believe me!" In her earnestness Cassie was unaware that she had called him by his given name. But it did not escape Steele's attention. Somehow it made her more vulnerable, more in need of protection.

"I truly have no place to go. I checked out of the hotel, believing that I would be joining Paul on his boat and that we would be sailing. Besides, there are no more rooms at the hotel. The clerk didn't charge me for tonight because he said they had a waiting list and that my room would be booked with no problem."

"Well, that's too bad," Steele returned, though his voice showed no sympathy. "I'll just take you to another hotel."

"But you can't do that, either," Cassie told him simply.

"And why can't I?" Steele's black eyebrow rose in question.

"Because I haven't enough money for a room," Cassie replied in a low, sad voice.

"I'm sorry about that, Cassie, but it doesn't change anything. I'll pay for your room because you're not going with me, and that's *that!*" His words had a ring of finality.

But Cassie was desperate and wouldn't give up so easily, she *couldn't!* She would *not* be deserted by another Malone, she vowed to herself.

"Steele, you *have* to take me with you, *you just have to!*" Cassie told him flatly, lifting her small chin defiantly.

"You're dead wrong, Cassie, I don't have to do anything of the sort."

"But Paul has deserted me, your own brother! I have no money, I know no one here, and I have no place to go. I sold my car, all my jewelry, and what furniture I had and gave the money to Paul to—"

"Oh, my God, you didn't!" Steele stared at Cassie in utter disbelief.

The report which Fred Hall had given him stated that Cassie Layton had sold her belongings and Fred had told Steele the same thing. But what Steele had not known was that his brother had been the recipient of the proceeds of that sale.

"But I did! Paul said we needed the money, that we would go to Nassau and would be married. But when we got here, he said we still didn't have the money we needed to start a life together so he began gambling, trying to win enough money. He made a lot of promises,

31

but kept none of them." Cassie's last words were a mere whisper.

"Why did you believe him?" Steele asked quietly.

"For two reasons. I thought he was honest and I believed he loved me!"

"You little fool! God, you little fool!" Steele groaned feelingly, his face an angry red. He shook his clenched fist in the air and gritted, "Damn you, Paul Malone! Damn you!"

Cassie sat very still, not able to understand this unexpected and, to her, unreasonable fury toward his brother. It was *she* who should feel all the anger, she thought, but she didn't venture to ask any questions. After a few minutes, Steele turned to her with a pleading look in his smoky gray eyes.

"Cassie, please try to understand. You will have to trust me when I tell you that you can't go back with me." He shook his head and sighed, sinking heavily into the chair. "There's just no way that I can take you with me. This is no place for you. Besides," he added savagely, "I have my own problems and responsibilities, without taking on those of my *dear brother!*" His last two words were bitterly sarcastic.

"Please, Steele! Please! I have to go with you!" Cassie had reached the end of her endurance. Her ankle pained and her nerves were frayed. She began to sob, tears staining her cheeks. "I'll do anything, *anything*, if you will take me!" she cried desperately.

Suddenly remembering the few dollar bills which she had surreptitiously taken from the remaining three hundred dollars and had tucked away in the bottom of her bag, Cassie groped underneath the outsized flannel shirt for the purse which still hung on her shoulder. Frantically, she rummaged through it.

"Here!" she exclaimed, drawing forth a handful of crumpled bills. "Here! Take it all!" Cassie tossed the bills at Steele when he made no move to accept the money. "Seventy-five dollars! It's all I have, all I kept for myself. It should help toward my keep!"

But when Steele only stared at the money that lay scattered on the floor, she cried out in desperation, "Take it, Steele, please take it!"

"No, Cassie. I'll not take your money," he replied calmly, shaking his dark head negatively.

"Then I'll work! I'll work for my keep! I'll do anything, Steele!" In her anxiety Cassie rose quickly from the bed, but as her feet found the floor, the persistent pain of her ankle caused her to sway.

With outstretched hands Cassie groped to steady herself and, with one long stride, Steele had reached her, once more to clasp her small frame with firm, yet gentle, hands. As she turned her forlorn face up to him, bright tears swam in Cassie's warm brown eyes and spilled over to run down her pale cheeks.

"Please, Steele, I'll do anything!" she whispered brokenly.

"Anything?" he asked huskily, suddenly gathering Cassie into his strong arms. The warm feel of her body, the soft, upturned lips were too great a temptation and before Cassie could answer his question, Steele's lips claimed hers.

Cassie's lips parted beneath his and Steele plundered their sweetness. It was not a flutter of passion that passed between them but a thunderbolt of desire as each hungered for the other.

Cassie's senses reeled and she felt an unfamiliar tightening within her stomach. As she melted to Steele's embrace and the kiss deepened, she felt as if she were drowning. Then suddenly Cassie realized that, though it felt so right to be in this man's arms, it was wrong and she must pull free.

"N—no," Cassie stammered. "No! Not *anything!*"

With her outspread hands against Steele's broad chest, she pushed at him to no avail.

Staring down at Cassie's kiss-bruised lips, flushed face, and passion-glazed eyes, Steele saw her small frame quiver slightly as he ran a warm hand along her upper arm. She had felt something, he was certain of it, she hadn't faked that response. She had been pliant in his arms, her lips had answered his.

A slow, dangerous fire was rising within Steele's body, a fire that he was sure that only this slip of a girl could extinguish. He wanted her. God, how he wanted her! But Steele had never forced a woman and he had no intention of starting now.

The silent plea in Cassie's gentle brown eyes caused Steele's arms to loosen their hold, breaking the suspenseful moment. It was not the quickening in his loins but in his heart that caused his reaction to Cassie's low words.

"Please, Steele, take me with you," she whispered pathetically.

With a deep sigh, Steele again gathered Cassie into his arms, more gently this time, and laid her upon the large bed. With wide, wary eyes, Cassie watched the man cross to a closet and return with a light blanket which he spread over her, his strong capable hands tucking it securely about her.

"Go to sleep, Cassie," Steele murmured. "We leave at daybreak."

With that he turned off the lamp and left the room, closing the door softly behind him.

Cassie lay for a long time, staring into the darkness. Sleep would not come easily to her. Sighing, she rolled over on her stomach, thrusting her hands beneath her pillow in an effort to make herself more comfortable. But within seconds she was tossing restlessly in the wide bed.

"What's wrong with you, Cassie Layton?" she asked herself aloud. "Your immediate problem has been solved, you're on your way back home. You should be content! And from this moment on, just take one day at a time."

Turning her thoughts to Paul, Cassie tried to remember all the happy hours she had spent with him, all the plans they had made. She tried to reason out why he had lied to her, why he had walked out without a word. But each time she tried to recall Paul's handsome face, it was the face of Steele Malone that emerged within her mind.

In total exasperation, Cassie breathed deeply. Immediately her nostrils were filled with the scent of Steele, the aroma of tobacco tinged with a hint of liquor, and the musky odor that was all his own. Running her hand over the smooth sheet that held the distinctly pleasant redolence of Steele Malone, Cassie felt a breathtaking shudder claim her. There was definitely something about this man that both frightened and excited her.

Shaking her head violently, Cassie reprimanded herself. "No! Please, no," her whispered plea filled the empty room. "I'll not play the fool again!" Her urgently whispered words seemed to mock her from every corner of the darkened room. She promised herself that, with Steele's help, she would find Paul and learn from him why she had been placed in such an awkward position. Furthermore, she firmly decided, she would make Paul pay for what he had done to her!

Gradually Cassie realized that the rain which had begun as a slow, fine mist was now falling steadily, and the tranquil rhythm lulled her into a fitful sleep. She dreamed of Paul, how she had loved him, and wanted only him. Paul, with his dark blue eyes.

In her dream Cassie ran across the sun-bleached sand toward her lover. As she reached him, his strong arms encircled her, crushing her to the length of his rock-hard body. His lips closed over hers and she relished the savor of his kiss.

The surf beat about their feet, sea gulls swept gracefully across the blue sky, and the warm, salty breeze stirred about them. It was the most wonderful feeling Cassie had ever experienced, it was heaven! She completely abandoned herself to this man who held her in his embrace, raising her dreamy brown eyes to his, wanting to capture the love within their depths. But the eyes which met hers were not dark blue. They were a cool clear gray. The smile on his lips wasn't the full-lipped smile of Paul but the disarming, crooked smile of Steele Malone!

2

~~~~~~~~~~~~~~~~

Cassie awoke with a start to the shrill whistle of the wind whipping about and the pounding of heavy rain beating against the boat. She felt the powerful surge of waves as they slapped with the fury of the sea. The room was in darkness, only the glare of lightning illuminated Cassie's surroundings in brief, but rapid, flashes. The compelling crash of thunder brought her upright in bed.

"Geez!" Cassie choked as she steadied herself with an outstretched hand. Another explosive clap of thunder caused the frightened girl to dive beneath the rumpled bedclothes, burying her head under her pillow as the thunder rumbled away into the distance.

Cassie had always been afraid of storms and as a small child she would flee to her parents' room. There she would nestle close and feel the security of not being alone. It had always helped but had never quite made the fear go away.

Now she remembered that Steele Malone was somewhere on the boat. Trembling, Cassie eased herself from the bed and stumbled through the darkness, searching for the door. She was guided by intermittent bursts of lightning. Just as she found the door knob, a blinding blaze of lightning flooded the room and again the thunder spat forth its wrath.

Terrified, Cassie jerked open the door and fled across the narrow hall as if the devil himself were at her heels, unmindful of her injured foot.

"Mr. Malone!" she screamed in a fear-gripped voice. *"Steele!"*

Running into the next room, Cassie's panic-filled eyes quickly searched for Steele, but to her dismay he was not there. A tiny light was burning on the chart table built into the wall and she knew that she was alone! Where could he be, she wondered, where could he have gone in this storm?

Brroooom! The violent roll of thunder echoed across the water and the boat lurched threateningly. Cassie braced herself in order to maintain her balance. She closed her eyes tightly and bit hard on her lower lip.

"I'm not afraid! I'm not afraid!" she whispered repeatedly, trying vainly to convince herself.

Suddenly a louder-than-ever, more forceful boom of thunder crashed nearer and, with her back against the wall, she crouched panic-stricken. And that was the way Steele found her when he came in. Stepping inside the doorway of the cabin with Cassie's luggage in hand, her shoes under his arm, and his yellow slicker drenched, Steele's gaze rested on the girl cringing on the floor.

Dropping his burden on a nearby bench, Steele made his way to Cassie with one long stride and knelt before her.

"Cassie! Cassie, what is it?"

Lifting frightened brown eyes to meet the concern in

Steele's gray ones, Cassie found she couldn't speak. The words seemed to be locked in her throat as her small body trembled uncontrollably. At another clash of thunder, Cassie flew into Steele's strong arms, burying her face against his chest as his arms encircled her.

"Is it the storm, Cassie? Are you afraid of the storm?" he asked gently.

Cassie nodded mutely and Steele's grasp tightened about her. Lifting her from the floor, he crossed to the cushioned seat at the side of the saloon and seated his large frame. He cradled Cassie on his lap and rocked her as if she were a small child as he spoke in low, soothing tones.

"There is no need to be afraid, Cassie," he began. "It's only rain . . . a little wind and a hell of a lot of noise." Chuckling aloud, he settled himself more comfortably and continued. "A storm is always worse on the sea, sometimes fierce, sometimes vicious, and at times can be frightening. It's as if she's built up a lot of anger and kept it suppressed for so long that finally it must be released."

Stroking her silken honey-colored hair, Steele calmed Cassie both with his words and with his gentle touch.

"You're a woman, Cassie," he went on, "and you should understand. The sea has emotions, too! Like a woman, she is beautiful and serene. She can be gentle, wistful, and even mysterious." Pausing, Steele took a deep breath. "But then again, like a woman, she can be hard, complex, and sometimes dangerous," he finished in his low, vibrant voice.

Cassie stirred and, looking up at the handsome face above her, studied the relaxed features, the sensual mouth curved in a slight smile.

"You—you make it all sound so simple . . . so lovely . . . and not at all frightening," she whispered wonderingly. "Is there nothing you're afraid of, Steele?"

The simple, honest question caught Steele off guard.

But the hammering of his heart as he held Cassie close reminded Steele of the yearning he had had for this gir when she had responded to his kiss with such passion.

That alone was enough to frighten a man like Steele Malone! Never had a woman affected him the way Cassie did, never before had his emotions been stirred to the extent to which she stirred him. This was not mere physical desire, he realized, but something much deeper —and frightening!

What was it about Cassie Layton? Even knowing that the woman he held in his arms had been his brother's mistress, and perhaps still loved the no-good bum, Steele could not deny that he himself wanted her.

"Well, isn't there?" Cassie repeated her question.

"Isn't there, what?"

"Isn't there anything you're afraid of?" she asked softly.

As his gray eyes burned into her, Steele replied in an easy, velvety voice that made Cassie's body feel warm and tingly.

"Oh, yes, little one, there is most definitely something that frightens me!" Steele answered seriously. Then, with a laugh of pure merriment, he added, "You see, I believe that all men, no matter how strong, share the same fear."

"And what is that fear?" she queried.

"This is not the time to tell you, Cassie," Steele answered carefully. "No, it most assuredly is not the time!"

For a brief moment Steele gazed into Cassie's trusting brown eyes and she was certain that she felt a faint tremor run through him. He must be cold, she thought, for he was still in his wet slicker. Tiny droplets of water glistened in his black hair like sparkling diamonds. Cassie watched as a raindrop slowly coursed its way down the length of Steele's cheek and, without thinking, she reached up and tenderly brushed it away.

As her hand touched his cheek, Cassie distinctly felt the shudder which ran through Steele's body and at the same moment felt a wave of emotion wash over her own. This was a sensation unfamiliar to her, and she thrilled at the breathless excitement which kindled deep within her.

Steele's large hand grasped Cassie's as her fingers trailed, feather-light, down his cheek. The warmth from his touch seemed to spread from Cassie's fingers down to her toes. Their eyes met, silently searching, and quite without warning Cassie's heartbeat changed its tempo.

"But, see here!" Steele's husky voice broke the lengthy silence. "I'm getting you all wet!" He laughed shakily as he lifted Cassie from his lap to the cushioned seat beside him. "It's a hell of a night out there," he said, standing and removing the wet slicker.

Cassie sat watching as Steele moved to the locker and hung up the raincoat. "I went out to get your bags . . . thought you might need something from them," he was saying, "and when I came back I found these on the deck." He lifted her sandals from the bench where he had dropped them. "Guess you lost them when you were stumbling around topside earlier."

Realizing that Steele was rambling on in an attempt to ease the tension which had built up between them, Cassie spoke hurriedly. "Th—thank you. You . . . you really didn't have to go to the trouble . . . I—I mean, with the storm and all." Her words came jerkily, as if she had trouble catching her breath.

Steele turned worried gray eyes toward her. "Are you all right?"

"Yes, f—fine." She managed a wavery smile as a shiver passed through her. "Just somewhat chilled." Cassie would never admit that her trembling was not caused by being damp or cold, but from the mere presence of Steele Malone. "But you're right, you did g—get me wet," she explained lamely as she stood up, hugging her arms about her. "I think I'll change into something warmer."

She made to pick up her luggage but Steele reached down at the same time, his hand closing over hers as she gripped the handle.

Without looking at him, Cassie said in a near whisper, "I can manage."

"Oh, but I'm a gentleman, Miss Layton, and a true gentleman would never stand by and allow a lady to carry her own luggage, now would he?"

Steele was so close to her that his warm breath fanned her flushed cheek, sending little electric shocks up her spine. He had made no move to stand aside, and Cassie was uncomfortably aware of his nearness and of his hand that still covered hers.

Then, with his free hand, Steele cupped her chin and tilted her face upward as his gray gaze held her mesmerized. Slowly his thumb traced her parted lips.

"Never deny a gentleman his rights, Cassie."

The unreadable mystery in the depths of Steele's now smoky gray eyes, the closeness of his body, and the low, hushed tone of his voice entranced Cassie.

"I—I'd like to . . ." she stammered, her words trailing into silence.

"You'd like to do what, Cassie?" Steele's dark eyebrows were raised in question. His lips were curved in a quiet smile.

Cassie swallowed hard. "I would like to change clothes," she managed and Steele's hand dropped from her chin. With a half-smile he picked up her bags and took them into the bedroom.

When he returned Cassie was still standing in the spot where he had left her, but before he had a chance to speak, she slipped by him with a murmured, "Thank you."

She closed the door after her, quite unaware that the

man she left behind stood for a long time, staring at the closed door, a thoughtful smile touching his lips. Then turning to the cushioned couch, Steele dropped his tall frame upon it and, with a deep, ragged sigh, clasped his hands beneath his head and tried in vain to sleep.

Cassie placed a small brown leather bag on the bed, snapped the latch, and opened the case. Then she stood, unmoving, as she wondered why the man had gone out in such weather to collect her belongings. Considering the storm, why had he not waited until morning? Steele Malone was certainly a far different kind of man than she had expected.

Seating herself upon the low bunk, Cassie began unbuttoning the checkered flannel shirt and remembered how gentle Steele's hands had been when he had cared for her ankle, how gentle he had been a little while before when she had been so afraid.

With a start Cassie realized that Steele Malone was fast becoming a danger to her! She was greatly attracted to him, attracted in a way that she had never before been to any man. She had thought that she loved Paul, had wanted to marry him. What had happened in the past few hours had changed all that. She had seen Paul for the sort of person he really was, had recognized that he was a mere boy compared to his older brother!

Steele had told her that Paul was no good, incapable of love, and that he was already married. Was that the man she had thought she loved, Cassie wondered. How could she? Suddenly she felt embarrassed, ashamed that she could have been such a fool!

One clear look at Steele, her brief association with him, his words of criticism of Paul which rang with truth, had shown Cassie what a scoundrel Paul really was. He was a hollow, shallow person and it was with relief that she felt all emotional ties ebb away, as surely as the snow melts beneath the rays of the sun.

It was over! Gone! All the affection she had nourished for Paul had died between one moment and the next. It seemed unbelievable to Cassie that emotions such as she had thought she had felt could die so quickly, so completely, so absolutely. However, she could not deny that it had happened.

But what was happening to her now? Her body, her mind, and even her young heart were being steadily drawn to Steele. Oh, why did I have to meet him, she groaned inwardly. Why must it all have to be so confusing?

Cassie flung herself, face down, upon the pillows as a low moan escaped her lips. Then she raised her body to prop herself up on her elbows, her face buried in her hands. This time the moan came from deep within her and louder than before.

Moments later, an urgent knock sounded, and Steele's concerned voice came from the other side of the door.

"Cassie? Cassie, are you all right in there?" There was no answer and Steele spoke again. "Cassie, I thought I heard you call out." Still there was no reply. Now his voice became insistent. "Cassie!"

"It's all right, Steele . . . I was just having trouble with the latch on my nightcase."

"Well, do you need my help?"

"No! I mean, no, thank you. I have it, now."

Cassie held her breath, hoping that Steele believed her lame excuse. She heard his mumbled "okay" and his departing footsteps before she released her breath with a slow sigh.

She had just begun to unpack when the sound of a radio drifted in from the outer room. The voice of the broadcaster became louder as Steele apparently turned up the volume. Although Cassie could not make out the words of the announcer, she sensed an urgency in his tone. Abruptly the radio was turned off.

She started at the quick knock on her door, accompanied by Steele's rumbling voice calling her name.

"Cassie, we're going to have to leave the boat, there are hurricane warnings. We'll have to go ashore." He paused and after a moment knocked again. "Cassie, did you hear?"

The door opened and Cassie stood wide-eyed, twisting her hands together nervously. "Yes, I heard," she answered simply.

"Get together a few things . . . enough for a couple of days," Steele told her as he crossed to the closet and began taking some of his own clothes from hangers. Pulling a well-worn duffel bag from the shelf, he stuffed the clothes into it. "I have a friend to whom we can go for shelter."

Steele was bending over a small seaman's trunk in the corner of the room, cramming more items into the bag. "I'll go topside and secure the boat while you get ready," he told her. Throwing the duffel over his broad shoulder, he walked to the door, stopping at the threshold.

Staring at the ashen-faced girl who stood in the center of the room, not moving, Steele began softly, "Don't look so frightened. This is only a warning. The storm is far out at sea but we will have high winds and heavy rains." He smiled reassuringly as he continued. "We wouldn't be safe or comfortable on this boat. Now, be a good girl and get your things together."

Cassie nodded silently, turning shakily to the task Steele had assigned.

Dressed in faded jeans, pullover sweater, and wearing a slicker from the boat, Cassie limped cautiously along the pier. She had been unable to put her shoe on because of the bandage on her swollen ankle. Rather than wear only one shoe, she had tossed both of them into her bag and gone out barefoot. In his haste to secure

45

the boat and get the two of them to safety, Steele had not noticed. Now, following a few feet behind her, he became aware that Cassie was not only shoeless, but limping noticeably.

Quickening his pace, Steele rapidly covered the short distance between them and, without warning, swept Cassie into his arms. Without breaking his stride, he continued down the pier, chuckling softly at her startled gasp of surprise.

Cassie huddled against Steele's broad chest as he made his way along the wharf toward the waiting taxi, the driver trudging only a few steps behind them, carrying their belongings.

As Steele placed her in the back seat and slipped in beside her, Cassie looked out the rain-splattered window. The wind had resumed its haunting howl and the rain its heavy downfall. She saw boats tossing and rolling with the swells of the water.

Looking up at Steele, Cassie saw that he was watching her, and in a small voice she asked, "What about your lovely boat, Steele? What will happen to it?"

With a slow smile Steele pushed back the slicker hood from Cassie's head and answered, "She should be able enough to ride out the storm if it isn't too bad. But now I have *two* ladies to worry about."

As if an afterthought, Steele whispered to himself, "And I can make no promises as to the future of either."

Although Cassie heard the murmured words, she knew instinctively that Steele had not meant them for her ears.

3

~~~~~~~~~~~~~~~

The taxi slowed, turned into the circular drive of an impressive high-rise condominium and slid to a smooth halt beneath the large canopy which stretched from the huge double-door entry across the driveway to form a portico.

Cassie knew that this building housed the wealthy of Nassau; she had seen it from afar several times since she had been on the island and had greatly admired its beauty.

As Steele paid the driver, Cassie wondered if he owned one of the apartments in this magnificent building but dared not ask questions. She knew that in her present near-penniless situation, she must depend on Steele and she had no intentions of prying into his private business.

Walking up the wide steps to the entrance, Cassie followed Steele's lead and removed her raincoat.

The doorman opened the massive door, touched his cap, and smiled at them.

47

"Evenin', Mr. Malone. Wicked night out, sir."

"Indeed it is, Henry," Steele returned in a friendly fashion, leaving no question in Cassie's mind that Steele Malone was well known here.

A bellhop trailed after them, carrying their luggage, as Steele led the way across the plush lobby area and stopped before highly polished elevator doors which opened noiselessly as Steele pressed the button. The speed with which they were carried upward positively took Cassie's breath away, and she grasped the brass handrail which ran the length of the car.

Stopping at one of the upper floors, the doors opened automatically and Steele stepped out, again followed by the silent Cassie and equally silent bellboy. No one had uttered a word since they had entered the building.

Directly across from the elevator Steele pressed a gold-rimmed pearl button set in the wall and Cassie heard a faraway musical tone as chimes sounded in a remote area of the suite before which they waited.

The door was opened by a pert maid dressed in smooth black silk with a tiny white Peter Pan collar and white cuffs. A wisp of ruffled apron encircled her small waist and her graying hair was in a braided coil low on her nape.

When she saw Steele, the maid stepped back, opening the door wide.

"Why, Mr. Steele, did you forget your key?"

"Yes, Letty, it seems that I did." Steele smiled, but it seemed to Cassie that he was somewhat embarrassed.

The bellboy deposited the luggage on the marble floor of the foyer. Steele turned and placed some money in the boy's palm. The young man backed out the door with a big grin and a departing, "Gee, thanks, Mr. Malone!"

"Who is it, Letty?" came the dulcet tones of a woman and Cassie, peering around Steele, saw the speaker sweeping across the large room toward them. She was simply but elegantly dressed in a flowing caftan the color of molten copper, and her perfectly coiffed blonde hair shone like soft moonlight.

Cassie was painfully aware of her own disheveled appearance, her wet hair pasted to her scalp, the oversized sweater hanging loosely from her shoulders, the faded jeans which she had rolled up to her knees, and her bare feet.

"Oh, Steele, *darling!*" the woman crooned, "I had heard the storm warnings and knew you'd come! Do take off those wet things and—" She broke off as her gaze darted to the small figure behind him. "Why, who in the world—"

Steele turned to Cassie. "Helen, this is Cassie Layton. Cassie, Helen Thorne." He pulled the reluctant Cassie forward, placing her directly in front of him, his hands resting easily upon her shoulders.

The woman's shock was more than evident. Her green eyes widened and she stared at the bedraggled Cassie as if she were a creature from another world.

"That—*that* is Cassie Layton? Paul's latest—why, she looks hardly old enough to—"

"Paul had to return unexpectedly to Miami, Helen," Steele cut in smoothly, "and I volunteered to see that Cassie is returned there safely." His thumb lightly traced Cassie's jawline as he continued with a short laugh. "But with the storm coming in I couldn't guarantee that safety on the boat so I brought her here."

Cassie suppressed a giggle as she watched the play of emotions in the jade green eyes staring at her. Why, she thought, the woman doesn't know whether to be disdainful or sympathetic. But at that moment definite hostility gleamed from the green orbs as they noted the tenderness with which Steele continued to stroke Cassie's damp

MAKE NO PROMISES

cheek. And Cassie sensed immediately that this woman
would be a bitter enemy.

The forgotten Letty stepped forward, breaking the
sudden tension.

"My, my, the child's clothes are damp and she must be
chilled," Letty clucked as she reached to pick up Cassie's
bag. "And barefoot, to boot! What's this?" Letty glared
at Steele towering above her. "She has an injured foot
and you're lettin' her stand here like this! Come along,
Mr. Steele, pick up the mite and bring her upstairs. I'll run
a hot bath and get her into some dry clothes." Fully
expecting her orders to be carried out, the feisty little
woman headed for the stairway.

"Yes, *ma'am!*" Steele saluted the departing Letty
and, lifting the astonished girl in his arms, followed the
maid to the upper floor.

Cassie was deposited upon a king-sized bed and sat
watching as Steele gave Letty a loving hug, told her to
"take good care of Miss Layton" and left the room,
pausing at the door to give Cassie a reassuring smile.

The maid disappeared into an adjoining room and
soon Cassie heard the sound of running water and
Letty's voice humming a lilting tune. She decided that
she could become quite fond of the older woman and
wondered how someone with such a sunny disposition
could work for the cold and haughty Miss Thorne.

While she waited for Letty to return, Cassie leaned
forward and unwound the wet bandage from her ankle.
Then she straightened and looked about the comfortable
room with high windows draped in rich shades of blue
that complemented the pale blue walls and the luxurious
off-white carpet. The furniture was in an antique white
with gold trim. It seemed to the lonely girl that the
gentleness of the room reached out to her.

How could a woman like Helen Thorne have decorated such a pleasant room, Cassie wondered. She had not appeared to be a person with soft, subdued taste. Cassie had considered Helen a flashy, flamboyant individual and, although she had been elegantly dressed, Cassie felt that Helen wore far too much makeup. The garish shade of red polish on her overly long nails and the honey-sweet voice which dripped with false sincerity brought to Cassie's mind the one word which she thought best described the woman—artificial!

Letty entered from the bathroom drying her hands on a hand towel, her kind face flushed with exertion.

"Now, missy, your bath is run and just right to the touch," Letty began as she helped Cassie off with her sweater. "I put a few drops of scented oil in the water and laid out two nice large towels." As she spoke, Letty flung the damp garments over one arm and handed a black silk dressing gown to the disrobed girl who stood uncertainly before her.

"But this isn't my robe, Letty," Cassie said hurriedly.

"I know, child. It belongs to Mr. Steele but he has more than enough around here and he won't miss this one. Now, put the thing on and go get your bath, honey."

"But—" Cassie began.

"Scat! Your bath water's gettin' cold!" And with that Letty started out of the room, calling over her shoulder, "I'll see to these wet things along with Mr. Steele's and be back shortly." The last few words were spoken as the door closed behind the woman.

Wrapping the silk robe closely about her, Cassie picked up her overnight case and crossed to the bathroom. She stopped short with a quick intake of breath at the sight of the elaborate bathroom. She had never seen one so lovely except in magazine advertisements.

The room bore the same deep off-white carpet as the rest of the suite and, in keeping with the adjoining bedroom, this room was in varying shades of blue. In the corner was a huge, oval sunken tub of pale blue, gold-veined marble with ornate fixtures resembling small, golden leaves. The faucet was a large, graceful golden swan.

Living ferns and ivies grew in brass pots and hanging baskets. The paper which covered the walls was an off-white color with tiny traces of soft blue velvet.

Dropping the robe, Cassie stepped into the warm perfumed water. She allowed her tired body to sink slowly into the pool and relaxed with a deep sigh. This was a world completely foreign to her, she thought, but since she had been thrust into it she was determined to enjoy it to the utmost.

As the weariness drained from her body, Cassie's mind turned to the events of the long day. Tears of exhaustion, confusion, and defeat trickled down her cheeks.

"You've got to go on," she whispered brokenly to herself. "You've got to build a future for yourself. Future!" Cassie bit out the last word. Future? Dear God, she groaned inwardly, there is no future now! Not with everything gone. No job, no car, no money . . . no *anything!*

Suddenly Cassie shook herself, both physically and mentally, and sat upright in the tub.

"Cassie Layton, get hold of yourself!" the girl chided herself. "You're no quitter, you never have been and you aren't about to start now!" With a tremulous smile she sank back into the water as her thoughts trooped on.

With Steele Malone's help I'll get back to Miami, she assured herself, and once there I'll just have to find another job and start over. It would be difficult, she knew, but she was determined that she would make it!

Finishing her leisurely bath, Cassie dried herself with one of the large soft towels that Letty had laid out for her.

She wrapped the other in a turban over her wet hair and padded across to the bedroom.

She lay back on the huge bed and took a deep sigh, her feet dangling over the side. What would happen next, she wondered curiously. Here she was in the home of one of Steele Malone's women and the haughty Miss Thorne didn't want Cassie Layton there. Somewhere, miles away at sea, a storm was churning into a hurricane and Cassie felt lost and unwanted.

Sure, Steele was around but the man didn't like the idea of her being here, she felt certain. Hadn't he told Helen Thorne that he had agreed to take her back home for Paul's sake? Actually, it was because he knew what Paul had done to Cassie and was only attempting to make amends. Yet Steele had been gentle, comforting and, even, she was convinced, had seemed to care about her. Or was he only tolerating her presence? Would he be relieved when he had seen her safely to Miami and feel that his responsibility ended there?

Would she ever understand Steele, Cassie wondered, would she ever really know him? Or did she want to? A man like Steele Malone was too complex, of that Cassie was sure. And to fall in love with him, or to care deeply for him, would be dangerous, fruitless, and disastrous.

He had destroyed her dreams of love and happiness, her hopes, her future. When he had told her the truth about Paul, Steele had barred Cassie from ever loving or trusting any man, ever again. At first she had hated Steele for telling her the things he had, for she felt that he had wrecked her life. Then she had realized that he had told her nothing but truth because he had no reason to want to hurt her, didn't even know her.

Cassie hadn't wanted to be attracted to Steele, but she again faced the truth and knew that she was. She had not reckoned with the desire, the yearning, that the tall handsome Malone would fire within her. But since he had held her close within the comfort of his strong arms, since that kiss which had become so unexpectedly ardent, despite the warring of her emotions Cassie was even at this moment longing for the man!

And now they were in Helen Thorne's beautiful suite, Helen Thorne, who knew Steele the way a woman knows her lover, had felt his arms around her, had tasted his lips, had—

"Stop it!" Cassie scolded herself aloud. "Just stop it! Steele Malone means nothing to you! *Nothing!*" Beating both clenched fists into the softness of the bed, she went on, "Steele is a means to get me back home and to help me find Paul." With a short, harsh laugh Cassie finished grimly, "And a means of having my revenge!"

"Do you often talk to yourself, missy?" Letty's voice startled Cassie. She sat up to see the maid coming into the room, a silver serving tray balanced on one arm. "Oh, you needn't look so put out, dearie. Old Letty talks to herself often." The woman gave a silvery-toned laugh which seemed contagious and Cassie found herself laughing with her.

"Mr. Steele thought you might like some tea," Letty said as she poured the hot liquid into a china cup and handed the cup to Cassie. "He had me put a few drops of brandy in to help you relax."

"Thank you, Letty. And please thank St—Mr. Steele for being so thoughtful." Cassie sipped the tea cautiously, then gave a satisfied, "Mmmm, good."

"I was glad to do it. You looked so lost . . . and afraid . . . when you first arrived. There's really no need to be uneasy, miss, you're welcome here."

"Oh, Letty, you've been so kind. I was a bit uncertain about imposing. I don't want to put anyone to any trouble. It is very nice of Miss Thorne to allow me—"

"Miss Thorne allow you!" Letty spluttered. "Whatever

does that woman have to do with it? Why, it's what Mr. Steele wants and that's the way it'll be!"

"But I don't understand, Letty. Isn't this Miss Thorne's home?"

"Why, no, miss! This is where Mr. Steele lives when he's on the island. He owns this whole building along with a few casinos and a hotel!"

"But he was on the boat when I went to find—uh—when I found him."

Letty's chuckle brought a puzzled expression to Cassie's face. Then she leaned forward and spoke conspiratorially. "Mr. Steele *always* goes there when *she's* stayin' here! He don't like possessive women and Miss Thorne certainly acts like she owns him!" Her brown eyes glinted and her lips were compressed.

"Oh, I see," Cassie said lamely, although she didn't, at all.

"Mr. Steele and her was to be married once. But that was a long time ago, only she won't forget it," Letty explained disgustedly. "But Miss Thorne has set herself out to get him back and she just might do it!" The little maid rolled her large brown eyes heavenward as she added devoutly, "God help us all if she does!"

Unreasonably, Cassie felt her heart drop in her breast. Why should it matter to her, she asked herself, why should Helen Thorne and her plans to snare Steele Malone bother *her?*

"Well, if it's what they both want," Cassie replied, trying to show indifference, "then we should wish them luck, don't you think so, Letty?"

"Humph!" was the only response as Letty headed toward the bathroom.

Cassie sipped her tea and found herself becoming drowsy. She set down the cup and released her hair from the towel, running her fingers through the thickness of the honey brown mane, then lay back on the soft bed. She was battling to keep her eyes open and strained to read the miniature numbers of the tiny gold-framed clock which stood on the bedside table.

"Twenty minutes 'til two in the morning?" Cassie's shocked voice met the keen ears of Letty as the maid returned to the bedroom.

"Yes, miss, and if you don't need me for anything else, I'll retire."

"Of course, Letty! Why, I had no idea of the time! I've had a most upsetting day . . . or evening, really . . . I'm sorry, please go on, I'm sure I can manage quite well." Cassie smiled sweetly. "And Letty, thank you for everything. You have been a comfort to me."

With an indifferent shrug and a kindly smile, Letty replied, "No need thankin' me for somethin' that was a pleasure to do. You see, I never had any children of my own and I enjoy mothering young ones. I came to work for Mr. Steele's parents when he was only three years old and my greatest happiness in life has been helpin' to raise that boy. And then, of course, young Paul came along a couple of years later." Chuckling softly, the older woman continued. "But anyone can see that Mr. Steele's my favorite and always has been."

"He must love you, too, from what little I have observed this evening. I wondered about the big hug . . . but that was earlier, before I learned that this is Mr. Steele's house and not Miss Thorne's. I thought you worked for *her!*"

"Oh, land's sakes, missy! I would *never* work for the likes of *her!* But enough of this chatter or I'll be here all night. Now you just go on to sleep. We'll have plenty of time to talk later."

"You're right, Letty. Good night, I'll see you in the morning."

"And good night to you, missy. Sleep well."

4

~~~~~~~~~~~~~~~

Still raining," Cassie murmured drowsily the next morning as she snuggled deeper beneath the overstuffed comforter of ice-blue silk. The drumming of the incessant rain did not bother her at all. It was the lightning and the fierce roll of thunder that so often accompanied rain that frightened her.

She had slept peacefully, but she seemed vaguely to remember that someone had entered her room once, or possibly twice, during the night. Cassie smiled sleepily as she remembered that Steele had instructed Letty to put brandy in her tea last evening, and it certainly had been effective! She could not remember any time when she had slept through a storm.

Cassie stretched leisurely, then casually glanced at the bedside clock. With a start she read the time to be half-past eight, and at that precise moment the aroma of brewing coffee reached her nostrils. As she sniffed the pleasant fragrance, the scent of frying bacon merged with it.

Somewhat reluctantly, Cassie eased back the covers and swung her legs effortlessly over the side of the bed and sat upright. Running her fingers through her mop of tawny brown hair, she yawned widely as she stood. She tested her injured ankle carefully and found that there was little discomfort when she put her weight upon it.

From her overnight case Cassie retrieved her tooth-brush, comb, and a few other items and started toward the bathroom. Her footsteps halted suddenly as she heard a high-pitched, light tinkle of laughter come from the room next to hers, followed by a deep masculine voice. The words she could not hear, nor did she want to. Her heart seemed to tighten in her breast as if it had been squeezed harshly.

Cassie shook her head disgustedly as she realized that she had clenched her toilet articles tightly against her wildly beating heart.

"Don't be so surprised, Cassie," she said in a choked whisper. "You knew last night that Helen Thorne was one of his women. Letty said that the woman was trying to win Steele back." With a dry, mirthless laugh, Cassie murmured to herself, "What better way than in his bed!"

Her toilette complete, Cassie emerged from the bath-room dressed in jeans and a red and white checkered blouse of soft cotton which she knotted just below her full breasts, leaving her midriff bare. She seemed totally unaware that, in doing so, she accented the flatness of her belly and the gentle curve of her shapely hips.

Cassie walked over to the dressing table and swept her lush brown hair into a ponytail, tying the silken softness with a narrow white ribbon. She applied only a hint of brown shadow to her eyelids, a touch of mascara to her lashes, and a clear gloss to her lips. Without a second glance at her attractive image she started for the door.

MAKE NO PROMISES

Stepping into the hall, Cassie closed the door quietly behind her as she tripped lightly along. But as she made to pass the open door of the room next to hers, she paused and with one quick glance her eyes took in the rumpled bed and the black negligee tossed carelessly across it. This was where Helen had slept, Cassie surmised, and no doubt with Steele! She was surprised to find that the very thought of it caused her heart to ache.

The sound of a happily whistled tune reached her ears, and Cassie's brown eyes widened as Steele stepped from what must have been an adjoining bathroom with only a white terry cloth wrap hanging loosely about his narrow hips. His head was bent as he briskly dried his dark hair with a towel.

Cassie wanted to move before Steele saw her but her feet refused to respond. Her gaze was drawn to his long, muscular legs, the flat stomach with a fine trail of dark hair disappearing beneath the wrap. His broad chest was tanned to a deep bronze, accented with a black mat of hair, now damp from his recent shower. The taut muscles in his forearms rippled freely as his hands deftly toweled his hair.

She slowly let out the breath she had unconsciously been holding and started to move away but the sudden movement caught Steele's eye.

The whistling broke off abruptly and a slow, almost lazy smile curved his sensuous lips as Steele's clear gray eyes held Cassie spellbound. Slowly he draped the towel around his neck, his tanned hands holding onto the ends of the towel as he leaned against a tall chest of drawers. Neither spoke but Cassie was aware of the electrified atmosphere which surrounded them.

Steele surveyed the wide-eyed girl from her ponytail where tiny whispers of curls had escaped the confines of the ribbon to wisp lightly about her flushed cheeks and forehead, down to her firmly jutting breasts. His eyes

59

rested lightly upon the bare midriff and moved down the length of her shapely, jean-clad legs to her bare feet.

"I—I'm sorry," Cassie stammered, "I was . . . well, I . . ."

"There's no need to apologize, Cassie," Steele's lazy drawl interrupted. "I don't object to a beautiful woman observing me." Again came the slow smile which was characteristic of him.

Cassie felt her cheeks flame as the color rushed into them. "I was not observing you, Steele Malone! For your information, I was—" Cassie stopped short. What was she doing? She could have walked on past that open door but she hadn't. She realized with clarity that she had enjoyed watching Steele unaware, had actually received pleasure from the sight of his body, and had been immensely satisfied with what she had seen. She could not but admire the beauty of his masculinity and, dear God, she couldn't tell him that!

"Well?" Steele prompted in interest, his eyes never leaving hers.

Before Cassie could find an appropriate answer, Steele had crossed the room and stood before her in the hall. She was quite taken aback with the flood of emotion that surged through her and found herself wanting to reach out to touch the thick mat of hair which covered his chest. Cassie breathed in the fresh scent of soap mixed with musky aftershave lotion. He smells good, she thought, the odor seeming to fill her senses until she felt almost dizzy.

Steele folded his arms across his bare chest and assumed an air of waiting. Finally Cassie raised her head to look up at him, her breathing beginning to quicken its pace. Her golden brown eyes met his gray gaze, and she had the sensation of being carried along on the current of a warm, gentle breeze. She felt completely lost and cared not, at the moment, where the drifting tide might carry her as Steele grasped her shoulders and pulled her close.

Cassie stood transfixed and breathless as Steele's lips slowly and deliberately lowered toward her own. She thrilled at the excitement awakened within her being and closed her eyes, parting her lips to accept Steele's, but the kiss never came.

"Mr. Steele!" Letty's voice rang from the bottom of the stairway.

Steele's lips were only a heartbeat away from Cassie's, his breath warm upon her upturned face . . . but when Letty called out, Steele's head stopped its descent and, without moving, his head still bent to Cassie, he answered Letty in a husky yet controlled voice.

"Yes, Letty?"

"Breakfast is ready. Shall I see if Miss Cassie is up and if she'll be wantin' something to eat?" Letty returned in her merry tone.

"I'll check on Cassie, Letty, and we'll be right down."

Sighing heavily, Steele brushed Cassie's warm cheek with the back of his hand, sending a delightful tremor through her as he whispered, "There'll be another time." With a slow, disarming smile he held her from him, a hand on each of her shoulders, as he warned, "I never start anything that I don't finish! That, you can count on!" Steele's grin widened as he concluded, "It's my nature."

And with those words he turned away and, without a backward glance, crossed the bedroom from which he had come, taking a rust-colored shirt and beige pants from a chair on his way.

Cassie stood uncertainly for a brief moment, then made her way shakily toward the stairs. As she began her descent, she stared unbelievingly at Helen Thorne who stood as if rooted to the spot, partway down the staircase. The look with which the older woman impaled Cassie was venomous. The stormy green eyes shot daggers, and Cassie swallowed nervously as she realized that Helen had witnessed the scene with Steele.

As Cassie made to pass the woman, Helen's hand snaked out and gripped Cassie's upper arm painfully, digging long nails into the soft flesh as she hissed, "What is your game, Cassie Layton? Aren't you satisfied playing the part of Paul's tramp?"

Cassie pulled herself to her full height and, with her firm chin jutting determinedly, she replied with all the dignity she could muster. "I'm playing no game, Miss Thorne! And I am *not* Paul's 'tramp'—nor, for that matter, am I *anyone's* 'tramp'!" Cassie said coolly, stressing her words. Controlling her temper with an effort, she turned dangerously narrowed eyes to the woman's hand that held her and stated in a deadly tone, "You will do well to release my arm, Miss Thorne!"

"And if I don't?" Helen snapped heatedly as she purposely tightened her grip about Cassie's arm. "What will you do?"

"I rather think you wouldn't wish to find out!" Cassie said dryly, and the expression in the depths of her brown eyes caused Helen to let go and stand back. Cassie passed the irate woman and proceeded down the stairs toward the kitchen, her head held high, her spine straight and proud. She would not fight with Helen, nor would she exchange words with the likes of her, Cassie determined. If, indeed, Steele Malone *did* belong to Helen Thorne as the woman claimed, then Steele was not the man whom she, Cassie, thought him to be at all. For Steele seemed to be his own man, his own master.

Cassie found Letty standing next to the long butcher block counter in the center of the kitchen, her hands on her hips, lips compressed into a thin line as she tapped the toe of her foot purposely on the stone-tiled floor. Letty's usually kind face was an angry red.

"Good morning, Letty," Cassie spoke cheerfully as she reached for a cup and saucer. "Mmmm, something sure smells good."

Letty said nothing but proceeded with her impatient foot tapping. Cassie tried again to make conversation.

"Is that cinnamon rolls I smell? I certainly hope so, they're my favorite."

"The witch!" Letty exploded. "She had no right! No right at all! Why, the nerve of that woman!" she fumed.

Cassie said nothing as she was surprised at the hostility the housekeeper exuded. From what little she had seen of Letty, she found this to be most uncharacteristic of the woman.

"Don't look at me like you don't know what I'm steamed up about, miss!" Letty went on, her voice a harsh rasp. "I heard it! I saw the whole thing!"

Cassie's hand stopped in midair, the coffeepot hovering over her cup, which rattled loudly on the saucer that cradled it. What had Letty seen? "I saw the whole thing," was what she had said. The scene with Helen? Or the scene with Steele? Or both? Letty must have read the questions in Cassie's eyes, for the next words answered her questions.

"You and Mr. Steele in the doorway. I saw what was going on. I was on my way up to call you to breakfast when I turned around to see that Thorne woman starting up the stairs behind me. I called out to warn you."

"Warn me?" Cassie asked in surprise. For some reason she thought Letty was upset about seeing her with Steele, his near-embrace, his state of undress.

"Yes, warn you and Mr. Steele. That woman would have made a spectacle of herself that would have been most embarrassing for you and would have caused Mr. Steele to lose his temper. He wouldn't have stood for it! So I thought it best to call out," Letty explained. Then her face brightened with a smile as she went on:

"I like you, miss, and you're good for my Mr. Steele. You're not like that Helen Thorne with her mightier-than-thou airs. She don't love that boy! All she wants is the Malone name and the prestige that goes along with it . . . not to mention the money!" Letty's kind brown eyes were tiny slits.

Cassie opened her mouth to say something, to change the subject, but she found that the little woman was not yet finished.

"And Mr. Steele *don't* belong to her like she claimed. Mr. Steele belongs only to Mr. Steele! That's been her trouble all along. Steele Malone's a man like his name. He can't be bent nor twisted 'round her little finger like she wants him to be! There was a time when she thought her charms worked on him." Letty shook her graying head. "Now she sees you for the threat you are!"

"Threat? Me?" Cassie gaped at her in utter disbelief.

"Yes, miss, you! Miss Thorne is well aware that Mr. Steele never looked at her the way he looks at you." Letty's merry laughter suddenly rang out and her eyebrows climbed upward. "And that bothers her right good, it does!"

Crossing to the stove, the housekeeper removed a warm plate from the oven and began spooning fluffy scrambled eggs on it, then covered the yellow mound with strips of crisp bacon. She placed two lightly browned biscuits, one on each side of the plate, and turned to Cassie who was perched on a tall bar stool behind the long counter.

The girl's chestnut brown head rested on the palm of one hand as she stared pointedly at her coffee cup, the fingers of her other hand toying absently with the spoon laying on the counter top.

"I'll just put your breakfast on the dining table, miss. You may start without the others, if you'd like," the older woman broke the silence.

"Oh, no, Letty! Please. I'd rather eat right here—" Cassie turned warm brown eyes up at the housekeeper. "That is, if it's all right. I'm not much on formality and, besides, I'd enjoy talking with you while you work. If you don't mind," she added as an afterthought.

"Mind? Sakes, no! I don't mind. And you're welcome to eat wherever you please. Now Miss Thorne, she insists on her meals being served in the dining room when she's not asking for a tray brought to her room. That woman—"

Letty's words broke off and a tinge of red flushed her pale cheeks. Cassie turned to look over her shoulder to see what Letty was staring at. Her eyes met the smoky gray ones of Steele who was leaning casually against the door frame, his arms crossed over his broad chest, an easy smile on his handsome face.

Cassie's heart lurched in her breast and she felt a fluttering in the pit of her stomach. Why does he affect me this way, she groaned inwardly. What is it about this man that makes my pulse race uncontrollably, she wondered, and she felt hot and cold at the same time; her breathing seemed to be restricted. This man was a menace to her self-control, awakening desires she had not known existed. Her senses reeled as Steele moved toward her.

"Good morning, ladies." Malone's deep, velvety voice sent a delightful wave rushing through Cassie's very being. He stepped to the counter and swung one long leg over the bar stool as he seated himself next to Cassie. "I'd like a cup of that coffee, Letty."

Hurriedly reaching into the overhead cupboard, Letty stood on tiptoe to retrieve an additional cup and saucer. She placed both on the counter before Steele and poured the dark liquid into the empty cup, then stepped back and watched closely as Steele's eyes rested tenderly on the pretty young woman at his side. There was a profoundly thoughtful look in his gray eyes that spoke volumes to the woman who had helped to raise him from a child to the man he now was.

"Will you be joining Miss Thorne in the dining room, Mr. Steele?" Letty's query broke the silence.

"No, Letty, I think I'll keep you and Cassie company here in the kitchen," he replied in his usual carefree manner as he studied Cassie over the rim of his uplifted cup. Cassie felt the uneasiness that she always did when Steele looked at her with those dusky gray eyes.

What lay beyond them, she wondered, what was the depth of the man who sat beside her? Somehow Cassie instinctively knew that he possessed a passion so fulfilling, so completely and supremely accomplished, that when he made love to a woman she could only be left satisfied, yet always wanting more.

Cassie blushed as she remembered the way her body had responded to Steele's touch, how she had melted in his embrace and the sensation of his lips on hers. He had a power over her, a dangerous, magnetic pull, for no matter how hard she fought against this mysterious force she couldn't deny how her heart pounded when Steele was near her.

What disturbed Cassie most was that she was afraid Steele was aware of her inner battle, her state of confusion, the chaos which he had created. Why else would he give her that slow, knowing smile when he was near, or go out of his way to embrace her, his body demanding a response. It was wrong, these feelings she had for Steele, the yearning she experienced. It was all wrong!

Even now Malone's haunting gray eyes held her, his gaze idly roaming over her, though Letty stood nearby busying herself with getting his breakfast. Feeling definitely uncomfortable, Cassie nibbled on her now cold biscuit. She tried to show unconcern at Steele's closeness to her when his hand touched the corner of her lip.

"Sorry," he apologized with a hint of laughter as she jumped with a start. "You had biscuit crumbs on that desirable little mouth of yours."

Cassie's face flamed as she snapped in embarrassment, "You could have told me. I would have removed it!" She brushed her napkin nervously across her mouth.

"I'm sure you would have, but it was purely instinct to just reach out and brush it off," Steele defended as he moved closer to her. In a low voice, he asked, "Had you rather I'd kissed it away?" Again that slow smile.

"Certainly not!" Cassie returned heatedly, her wide brown eyes darting to Letty. But the woman had her back turned discreetly as she washed a large iron skillet at the double sink. However, Cassie had the distinct feeling that the woman had heard every word. Or did she only imagine Letty's shoulders moved with silent laughter?

Steele's annoying chuckle met Cassie's ears and she glanced back at him, her gaze meeting his. There was an unreadable message dancing in the depths of those memorable gray eyes.

"If you'll excuse me, I'd like to go to my room," she said quietly, her voice betraying only the slightest tremble. "I saw some books in the library as I came through. Would it be all right if I take one to my room?"

"Of course, you may do anything you like. Until this rain lets up you're going to have to occupy your time in some manner." Steele spoke in a controlled voice as he continued, "Now, as for me, I must get out in this damnable weather. I have several interests on the island and sometimes they present problems which demand my attention, fair weather or foul."

Malone unfolded his length from the bar stool and stretched his muscular arms high over his head in a curiously boyish fashion. Then he turned to Letty saying, "See that Cassie has a good lunch," and gestured to her still full plate.

"Thank you for your concern, Mr. Malone," Cassie said with a touch of sarcasm, "but I'm quite capable of taking care of myself!"

Steele's dark brow arched as he replied smoothly, "Oh?"

Cassie felt the hot blood flush her cheeks as she remembered that only the night before she had told him she "would do *anything*" if he would consent to take care of her and see her safely home. She had certainly not shown that she was "quite capable of taking care of herself," Cassie reminded herself disgustedly.

Cassie turned back to the counter and looked down at her breakfast. Then she raised pleading brown eyes to the housekeeper and said quietly, "Thank you, Letty, for the coffee and for the lovely breakfast. I'm sorry that I couldn't finish it . . . I—I guess I just wasn't very hungry."

"It's quite all right, miss, I understand," Letty assured her sweetly.

And she probably did understand, Cassie thought with candor. Had Letty become aware of how Steele affected her, she wondered? Had the older woman surmised that an invisible bond had sprung up between the two of them? She found herself wondering what the kind-hearted, motherly Letty would think of a relationship between Cassie and this man whom Letty looked on almost as a son.

Entering the large, wood-paneled library, Cassie made her way slowly around the room as she observed the rich furnishings of what was probably the favorite spot of the owner. She could easily imagine Steele seated behind the huge, highly polished mahogany desk with his dark, handsome head resting against the expensive leather of the wing chair.

It was a beautiful room and quite suited to its master, Cassie decided. Her wide eyes took in the walls covered with floor-to-ceiling shelves graced with an abundance of books of every description.

Running a slender forefinger along a row of books, Cassie read the names aloud. "Browning . . . Tennyson . . . Kipling . . ." she read as she moved along. There was an entire shelf of mysteries and western novels. Cassie hurried past them until her wandering eyes fell on a whole row of romance novels. Romance! Heaven forbid, she thought fervently. Then she chuckled aloud as she thought of her own unique, though unrealistic, romantic situation.

With a deep sigh, Cassie moved back up the rows of books, her hand coming to rest on a leather-bound volume of Browning. She decided that she needed no complicated plot, whether it be romance, murder, or whatever, and she probably wouldn't be able to read anyway. Her mind was too full of her own immediate problems—her confused feelings, the scene with Helen Thorne, the unsettling attraction she felt for Steele Malone and, she reminded herself, the unresolved question of her future.

Yes, Cassie mused, she would have plenty to occupy her time. Her thoughts alone would fill most of her waking hours and probably would invade her dreams as well.

Taking the volume of Browning from its place on the bookshelf, Cassie left the room and climbed the stairs to her room.

5

~~~~~~~~~~~~

Two days later Cassie stood staring through the rain-spattered window pane at the leaden skies. Two days of rain, rain, and more rain.

"When will this rotten weather clear up?" she muttered to herself. She was ready for blue skies, white clouds, and bright sunshine. Perhaps that would help the moodiness she had been experiencing for the past forty-eight hours, for she was not normally a moody person.

As she stood looking out at the sodden world outside, Cassie's thoughts turned inward toward her own situation, her problems, and the drastic change her life had undergone in the short period just past—only two days since Paul had deserted her and she had found Steele. Steele Malone, who had pulled no punches about telling her the bald truth about his brother.

Cassie realized that she barely thought about Paul

70

anymore, what he had done to her didn't even hurt—if it ever had, she thought, finally admitting to herself that she had felt only anger toward Paul!

Now she found that her feelings for Steele were much different from those she had had for the younger Malone and far stronger. How could she feel an attraction so strong, so quickly, for a stranger who was the brother of the man she had thought she loved, the man she had wanted to marry! It was because of these uncertainties, the new and strange aching desires, and because of the man Steele Malone that she couldn't sleep, couldn't eat, couldn't think!

Cassie sighed deeply and, turning from the window, glanced at the bedside table. The luminous dial of the clock showed the time to be half-past two in the morning. She must get some sleep. Yesterday morning Cassie had stared unbelievingly at the young woman who looked back at her from the mirror. That girl had a drawn, ashen face with noticeably dark circles under her large brown eyes and her naturally tinted lips were pale.

Was that looking-glass girl Cassie Layton? She couldn't believe it! What was happening to her? How could she have let herself get into such a condition when she had been a normal, well-adjusted person who had never before let anything get her down!

Drawing the tie of Steele's silk robe more securely about her, she padded across the bedroom to the door. Perhaps a glass of warm milk or a cup of hot tea would help her sleep, she decided.

When she started to pass the bedroom next to hers, Cassie paused momentarily and stared at the closed door. Her heart resumed its dull ache and hot tears threatened to scald her already burning eyes. They were probably there, behind that door, Cassie thought bitterly, entwined in each other's arms. She stood listening to the silence of the house. Only the faint sound of the steady downpour met her ears.

Closing her eyes tightly, Cassie swallowed the rising pain that swelled in her throat, nearly choking her. Why did it have to hurt so, she wondered. Her young heart had never had to contend with an all-consuming, bittersweet consciousness of true, abiding love before so Cassie did not yet realize that she had fallen in love. Never had a man touched her heart with sincerity and possessiveness mixed with passion, and Cassie found herself vulnerable to the longing inside her that had responded so strongly to Steele Malone.

As she made her silent way down the stairway, Cassie shook her head violently in an effort to wipe out the memory of Steele's lips on hers, his strong arms about her. "It felt so right," she whispered into the dark, "so very right!"

Halfway across the large living room, Cassie stopped short as a slight movement caught her eye. Her searching gaze rested on a tiny red glow in the darkness of the room. She stood rooted to the spot, watching as the ember suddenly glowed brighter, and within the sphere of its lumination she traced the handsome face of Steele. With that one fleeting glance Cassie's body started to tremble and her mouth went dry. The effect the man had on her was unnerving, frustrating, and maddening!

"Can't sleep?" Steele's smooth rich voice glided through the duskiness effortlessly. The velvety sound did not help her mental or emotional state.

Drawing a deep, unsteady breath, Cassie answered, "It . . . it's the rain, I guess. When will it ever stop?"

"Most likely it will be long after we're ready for it to stop," Steele replied candidly.

There was a faint rustling sound from where Steele sat in the shadows. Her eyes had grown more accustomed to the darkness, and Cassie saw his powerful frame silhouetted against the dim light of the window as he pulled the drape aside with one hand.

"Come here." The two-word invitation was soft and coaxing and it penetrated Cassie's reserve. She took a small unsure step forward, then hesitated.

"Come on, Cassie. Come and watch the rain with me. It's really quite beautiful, you know, and undisturbed tonight. Listen to it . . ." Steele's words trailed off into a near-whisper.

In the quietude of the room Cassie's ears adjusted to the pitter-patter of the rain-composed melody. For the first time she heard rain as a sweet, gentle rhythm. Never before had rain sung out an almost sad and haunting love ballad. It seemed to call to her, beckoning her closer.

Cassie stood at Steele's side, her warm brown eyes staring out into the gray night. Only faint, multicolored lights shimmered over the island far below the window, barely visible through the haze of the fine rainfall. Steele is right, she thought surprisingly. It *was* beautiful.

"Do you hear it, Cassie?" Steele's voice was hushed and his breath was warm upon her brow as he stood close beside her. "Can you hear the song it sings? Out there in the night . . . draping the land with its shroud of mist? There's no pale moon to creep slowly across the sky, no diamond-bright stars . . . only unseen shadows making their way along the windswept horizon."

He was almost poetic, Cassie thought. Then she caught her breath sharply as Steele slipped an arm about her narrow waist, bringing her into the circle of his embrace. Her senses reeled at the touch of his body and the heady masculine scent which assailed her nostrils.

"You can almost feel its loneliness and hear the passion." Steele's low voice did strange things to Cassie's emotions as he continued. "A song that is no more than a whisper upon the cool night breeze." He tightened his

73

embrace as he concluded, "Soft . . . sweet . . . seductive . . ."

"What is it, Steele, this song it sings?" Cassie asked quietly.

"It sings the song of forbidden love, a passion so great that it's unforgettable. A love struggling against the impossible!"

"But why? Why should love be forbidden? If it is so strong, it should be able to endure." Cassie's words were spoken with deep feeling. "Love should be allowed to grow, to flourish into . . . into something tender and lasting."

"You're fascinating, Cassie Layton." Steele released the drape, his hands caressing her shoulders as he turned Cassie to face him, drawing her even closer. "A warmth flows from you that is sweet and longing. The softness in those lovely brown eyes could destroy a man's defenses." Steele took a deep, ragged breath as he concluded, "You, little one, are a real woman! You are also a marvelous creature and a danger!"

"A danger?" Cassie echoed, her voice a soft, rustling sound.

"Oh, yes!" A low chuckle rumbled deep within Steele's throat. He cupped her chin in his hand and tilted her face upward. Even in the dusk Cassie could see the unreadable mystery in his gray eyes. "There's something between the two of us, my dear, something strong and dangerous. And I'd wager that you are as much aware of it as I!" The last sentence was a seductive whisper.

With a sudden passionate groan, Steele crushed Cassie against the length of him. His hands entwined in her silken hair and his mouth came down upon hers, his tongue parting her lips, teasing the corners of her mouth before taking complete possession.

The kiss was urgent, demanding, and Cassie felt the

rising tide surge deep within her, aware of every hard contour of his strong body. A tremor ran unbidden through her and a moan escaped her as her arms, of their own volition, encircled Steele's neck.

Yes! Oh, yes! her mind called out. There was a definite attraction between them. And this kiss was not just a passing fancy, she'd be a fool to try and deny it. To Cassie, it was the culmination of the long hours of frustration she had struggled through. Never in her twenty-one years had she experienced emotions such as those she felt with Steele Malone!

The kiss lengthened, drawing Cassie into depths of passion that frightened her. Yet she refused to be the one to end it, to let go of the excitement, to let go of the man! There was a dark and forbidden beauty in what she was now experiencing and she wanted to hold on to it for as long as she could.

Steele's hands left trails of fire down her throat and along her shoulders, coming to rest at either side. Then, taking the silk tie of Cassie's robe in one hand, he slowly released the silken belt and reached inside. As he ran skillful fingers over her soft flesh, he felt her shiver at his touch, felt the rapid rise and fall of her full breasts beneath his exploring hand.

"Oh, God, Cassie!" Steele's voice was a hoarse groan. "I want you! I need you!" he whispered against her lips. "God! I need you so much!"

Without warning Steele held Cassie away from him and for a breath-stopping moment they stared into each other's eyes. His gray gaze held her, their depths smoldering with rising passion.

"Let me make love to you, Cassie!" he whispered urgently.

Cassie felt herself yielding, she knew the same aching, the same unquenched thirst that Steele must feel. But before she could speak, his lips claimed hers once more.

She was lost . . . lost in his demanding force . . . she knew that she couldn't pull free, as Steele's knowing hands further explored the silken softness of her pliant body.

Struggling to keep her control, Cassie knew that her heart, her mind, and her body were all fighting a losing battle. She desired this man, this stranger. The very touch of him set her aflame, his caresses stirred her, his hands, tender, yet urgent, ran over her aching flesh. Steele's slow, gentle movements were coaxing her, sending Cassie deeper and deeper into an impassioned fever.

Even as her conscience silently scolded her, Cassie felt her robe slip from her shoulders to fall unheeded to the floor. No! The warning cry came from within her. *You are weak, Cassie Layton, what you are doing is wrong!* She felt confused—angry with herself for her wanton need for this man—yet it seemed the natural thing for her to be in his arms . . .

Cassie had not known at what point Steele had shed his own robe but now his naked flesh pressed ardently against hers. She felt breathless . . . light-headed . . . she was ablaze and fast losing control!

As their heated bare flesh blended, the entwined lovers sank slowly to the carpeted floor, Steele covering Cassie's body with the hard length of his own.

"You're beautiful, Cassie, more beautiful than I had imagined." Steele buried his dark head in the valley of her breasts. His breathing was ragged and unsteady. Then he raised his head and stared deep into the golden brown depths of her passion-glazed eyes as he spoke huskily.

"It may be wrong, Cass. Dear God, I don't know! All I am certain of is that I want you! I've wanted you since the first time I saw you—" He broke off and sighed deeply. Tracing a finger along her parted lips, he went on. "From the first time I kissed you and tasted those sweet lips I have never desired a woman as much as I desire you!"

Again Steele took her mouth in an almost savage kiss and, although demanding, it was sweet, warm, and moving. The heat of his passion kindled anew the fires burning within Cassie, and a need for fulfillment washed over her.

Her emotions were raw, laid bare, and Steele's lovemaking tempted Cassie to the roots of her soul. He was succeeding in awakening every nerve in her being and she was allowing herself to be swept away on the tide of passion . . .

Suddenly Cassie recalled the words Steele had whispered so tenderly yet urgently, "I want you" . . . "I need you" . . . But was that enough, she asked herself, was passion and desire enough? Steele Malone did not love her. He was only a man with the needs of a man, needs of the flesh. It went no deeper than that, the inner voice was telling her, but how she wished it did! That would make it all right, she was sure.

Even Steele had said, "It may be wrong." He had said that *he* didn't know. Dear God! She had no answer for it, either, and if both of them had doubts then what *was* the answer, Cassie thought desperately.

"Steele?" Cassie choked out the name with all the strength she could muster and with considerable control she forced back the delight of his lovemaking. Willing herself not to respond to his touch, she lay stiff and passive in his arms. "Steele, I—I can't!" she managed in a broken voice.

Steele's body became rigid as he lay unmoving upon Cassie's trembling form for a moment before rolling his weight to one side and, bracing himself on his elbow, stared questioningly into her flushed face.

"You want me! I'm not a fool, Cassie," he stated

knowingly. "You were eager for my kisses, my touch. *You want me—and I want you!*"

Cassie turned her face away so that he could not read the raw desire in her eyes. It would be her undoing, she thought. All he would need to do was to read the truth mirrored in them. She would be lost if he continued to kiss her, to touch her with such gentleness and, yes, even tell her once more that he wanted her. There would be no stopping . . . no turning back . . . until she had given to Steele Malone that which she had given to no man!

"Tell me, Cassie, tell me that you feel the way I do," Steele whispered to her in the darkness.

But she couldn't . . . she wouldn't! She'd not allow herself the hurt and emptiness she knew she would feel if she allowed Steele to possess her without love! She could never give herself to a man without some real commitment.

Even believing herself in love with Paul and actually planning to marry him, Cassie had always kept him at arm's length. Looking back, she realized that she had never had to keep a rein on her emotions because she had never before experienced the deep stirring of desire with Paul . . . not with anyone . . . only with Steele Malone.

No, Cassie decided firmly, she could not allow this man to fire her yearnings any further. She tensed, controlled her breathing, and gazed into his smoky gray eyes and spoke calmly.

"I am a woman, Steele, and I have emotions and desires just as you do." She swallowed with difficulty and closed her eyes to discourage the tears which threatened to spill over. "Yes," Cassie choked. "Yes, I admit that my body responded to you. But without my heart doing so, there would be physical pleasure, Steele, but no true fulfillment for either of us!"

78

"And where is your heart, Cassie?" Steele questioned in a cold voice that sent a chill up her spine.

She couldn't tell him, Cassie thought in sudden panic. She couldn't let him know that she was only throwing up a shield to protect herself from further hurt and frustration. No, she couldn't answer his question—not honestly!

Steele's strong fingers dug into the softness of her cheek as he forced Cassie to look at him. His eyes were a dark, stormy gray as he demanded:

"Answer me, Cassie!" The words came through tightly clenched teeth, and when she made no reply his grip tightened painfully and he continued. "Is your heart with Paul?" Still no reply. *"Is it Paul who has your heart?"* he spat venomously. "God, Cassie, answer me!"

That was it, she thought, her heart breaking. Paul could be her way out. She could use Paul as an excuse, a way to escape from the dilemma she was now caught in. She would tell Steele that she still loved his brother. Surely he wouldn't want her, thinking that she desired another!

Cassie drew a deep, uneven breath and gave Steele an answer.

"Yes! Yes, if you must know! My heart is with Paul!" she lied.

A dead silence claimed the room and Cassie suddenly felt afraid and unsure. Dear God! The rage that she could feel vibrating from Steele shook her to the very core of her soul. He was trying hard to control an explosive anger, she knew, an anger that went so deep as to be violent if unleashed.

With a sudden oath, Steele pushed Cassie from him and rose to his feet and retrieved his robe. He put it on and without another word stalked to a chair near the window. Sinking heavily into its depths, he leaned his head against the chair back and lit a cigarette.

Cassie fumbled in the semidark and found her own robe, wrapping it around her with shaking hands.

"I—I'm sorry, S—Steele," she whispered brokenly. "But you demanded an answer. I—I only—"

"You only told me the one thing I didn't want to hear!" Steele broke in bitterly. Pulling deeply on his cigarette, he exhaled a cloud of white smoke and watched as it drifted lazily across the room and was lost in the dimness. "I must confess that your straightforward honesty threw me, Cassie. I was conceited enough to think that I could be a better lover than my brother."

Steele laughed mirthlessly and added, "I thought I could wipe out Paul's memory and replace it with mine!"

"Steele, I—" Cassie hesitated, her heart winging across the space which separated them.

"Go to bed, Cassie," Steele said wearily. "Go back to bed and dream of your lover. Warm yourself with empty dreams and broken promises!"

Cassie rose on trembling legs and brushed the hot tears from her eyes before they could overflow and scald her already burning cheeks. She had literally cringed from the harshness in Steele's voice, but she would not retreat to the safety of her room as he had ordered her to do. And not as she wished to do.

Instead, Cassie proceeded to the kitchen which had been her original destination. She turned on the light above the stove and opened the refrigerator to remove a carton of milk.

Pouring the white liquid, Cassie filled the pan to the brim unthinkingly as her mind went back over the words Steele had spoken.

"Your straightforward honesty," he had said. *"Your straightforward honesty!"* Cassie groaned aloud as her mind repeated the words. Never before had she told such an outrageous, bald-faced lie! And Steele had believed her. Had taken the words at face value!

Placing the saucepan on the stove, Cassie adjusted the burner and spoke to herself in a low murmur. "All things are difficult before they are easy, Cassie!"

She knew that it would be a very long time before she would forget the events of this night! A long time before she could dismiss the passion and consuming desire she had found in the arms of Steele Malone! A very long time—if ever!

6

∞∞∞∞∞∞∞∞∞

I'm terribly worried about the child!"

Letty's concerned voice drifted up the stairs and met Cassie's ears as she stopped on the landing. She knew she shouldn't eavesdrop but curiosity held her to the spot and she waited breathlessly for the next words.

"Worried?" came the rumbling of Steele's deep voice. "Why, has something happened that I don't know about, Letty?"

"I don't know, Mr. Steele," Letty sighed worriedly. "The miss just isn't the same. She's changed, even though she's only been here a week. I can tell. She's not eatin' right and not sleepin' good. I've seen the light shining beneath her door in the wee hours of the night."

Letty paused briefly, as if to catch her breath, and began again.

"The mite looks downright peaked, if you ask me. And this morning when I went to call her for breakfast she said she felt dizzy and nauseous. Later I went up and took her some warm tea and dry toast."

"Nauseous! Dizzy!" The two single words boomed out, and Cassie wished she could see the expression on Steele's face as the words exploded from him. She noted that they were spoken as statements, not questions, and a smile tugged at the corners of her mouth as she realized what he must be thinking.

"Yes, Mr. Steele, there is definitely something very wrong with the child," Letty replied, and it occurred to Cassie that the woman had not caught the implication that Steele's voice and words conveyed.

There was a prolonged silence and Cassie wondered if they had left the room. For fear that they would come into the hall and find her standing there on the shadowy staircase listening to their conversation, she decided to descend as if she had not heard them. But as she took a couple of hasty steps downward, Cassie heard the clear mocking laugh of Helen Thorne and the barbed remark she threw at Steele.

"Oh, my darling! You don't suppose that the little dear has gotten pregnant!" Again her spiteful laughter rang out as Helen mused aloud, "I wonder how Paul will handle the news."

"Shut up, Helen!" came Steele's deadly command.

To Cassie the vibrant sound seemed to "rattle the rafters," as her mother would have said. Then her attention was drawn back as Steele's voice raged on.

"You will keep your comments to yourself. Do you understand?" His words were razor sharp.

"But Steele," Helen began, only to be cut off abruptly.

"I mean it, Helen! You've no right to accuse Cassie of something which you know nothing about!"

"Then I shall simply ask her!" Helen replied coolly.

"You certainly will not!" Steele roared emphatically.

83

That was her cue, Cassie thought. It was time to make an entrance, she had heard enough. Swiftly she ran down the remaining stairs and entered the living room, stopping dead in her tracks as she viewed the tableau before her.

Steele's roared ultimatum had brought Helen leaping from her chair to face the angered man. The two stood staring at each other mutely, stormy gray eyes clashing with burning green eyes in silent combat.

"And what is it that you wish to ask me, Miss Thorne?" Cassie's question vibrated across the still room and the two adversaries stood frozen for a moment. Then Steele's dark gaze slid to Cassie as Helen turned slowly about, apparently attempting to gain composure.

What about Steele, Cassie wondered, what was he thinking? His handsome features were covered with a mask of seeming indifference. Well, she wouldn't give him the satisfaction of knowing that *he* was the cause of her frustration. It was because of Steele that she had lost her appetite and suffered so much inner turmoil. Steele believed Cassie to be his brother's lover, so would it really make any difference if she denied Helen's accusation?

"Good afternoon, Cassie," Steele broke the stunned silence. "I hope—"

"What was your question, Miss Thorne?" Cassie repeated as if Steele had not spoken. She was pleased to see a flush touch Helen's cheeks at her persistence and was amused at the angry brick-red color which surged into Steele's face as he gritted his teeth, causing a tiny muscle to twitch in his jaw.

"Uh—" Helen attempted to find her voice but could not. She looked up at the tall man beside her as if for help. But when Steele showed no inclination to intervene, Helen tried again.

"Well, Letty mentioned that you weren't feeling well."

She paused and once again glanced up at Malone's rigid stance and, gaining no help from that direction, finished lamely, "And—uh—well, Steele and I were wondering what the problem might be."

"The *truth* of the matter, Helen, is that the two of you were *really* wondering if I am pregnant with Paul's child!" Cassie stated bluntly, as she watched the shocked expression on both their faces.

When neither Steele nor Helen responded to her statement, Cassie lifted her chin defiantly. "Whether or not I'm pregnant, let me assure you both that it is no concern of yours! So please don't worry yourselves in the least!"

And with that Cassie stalked from the room without a backward glance. The only sound was Cassie's retreating footsteps as she crossed the entry hall, followed by the loud slam of the heavy wooden door.

Once outside the suite, Cassie leaned her trembling body against the wall as she waited for the elevator. Repeatedly pressing the "Down" button, she muttered in agitation, "What right does Helen Thorne, or, for that matter, Steele Malone, have to question me about *anything!*"

With a mild oath Cassie willed the elevator doors to open. She felt that she *had* to get away for a while. She needed some time alone and glanced over her shoulder to make sure that Steele did not follow her.

Cassie breathed a sigh of relief when the elevator doors slid silently open to admit her and she was able to step into the car alone.

Walking along the sun-baked beach, Cassie sought the freedom of the out-of-doors. She reached down and rolled up the legs of her faded jeans about her knees, then removed her sandals to bury her toes deep into the golden sand. She breathed in the tangy salt air and shaded her eyes with her hand as she tilted her head upward to scan the aqua sky, noting with delight the white fluffy clouds which scuttled overhead.

Yesterday the rain had finally stopped and today was perfect, Cassie was thinking as her eyes rested on a small boat some distance out upon the clear blue-green surface of the water.

Watching the boat tossing gently upon the near-smooth water, Cassie saw two divers roll over the side and plunge into the depths. They must be searching for submerged coral reefs, she mused, moving on down the beach lost in thought.

Soon she found herself growing tired and stopped to rest. It was the lack of rest and her inability to eat properly, she thought with a grimace, which caused her to tire so quickly. She had always been strong and hearty, had enjoyed hiking, jogging, and bicycling and now, in just a few days' time, she had become a weakling, she thought with self-disgust.

With a heavy sigh Cassie sank to her knees in the soft sand and reached out to scoop the golden substance in her hand, letting the tiny, fine crystals slip through her fingers.

Her mind wandered back over the week since she had stumbled into the life of Steele Malone. Only one week and she had gone through so many changes, most of them emotional. Of one thing she was certain—she had done considerable "growing up" in a very short time!

Cassie sighed, letting the memories float back, the touch of Steele's hands on her flesh, his kiss. There had definitely been something flowing between them that night. Cassie shook her head in exasperation, suddenly weary with the effort of trying to figure out a solution to all the problems.

Cassie was so engrossed in her thoughts she neither

saw nor heard the approach of the man who spoke to her. Startled, she turned toward him.

"Sorry, I didn't mean to frighten you." He had a warm, pleasant voice. "I saw you from the boat through my binoculars," the man said easily. "I hope you don't object." He flashed a boyish grin.

Cassie noted that he was wet, droplets of water shining on his tanned body. In his hand he held a pair of large black flippers and a diving mask was pushed high on his blond head.

"Oh, were you on that boat?" Cassie queried, pointing to the small craft still tossing gently about on the ocean.

"Why, yes, I was." He dropped the flippers to the sand and asked, "Mind if I join you?"

"Of course not. Please do." Cassie smiled up at the man, completely unaware of the lovely picture she presented sitting there in the sand.

"My name's Troy Warner," he said casually as he removed the mask and seated himself near Cassie.

"Cassie Layton."

"And what would a pretty young lady like you be doing alone on this near-deserted beach? I've been watching you for quite some time now from out there." Troy nodded his sun-bleached head in the direction of the boat.

"And what were you doing out there—looking for buried treasure?" Her eyes turned to the small plastic pouch hanging from a loop on Troy's swimming trunks.

"This?" Troy held the bag up, then with tanned fingers unhooked the pouch from where it rested on his slim hip. "Well, it is treasure to me." He emptied the contents onto the smooth sand between them, naming each item as he pointed it out. "This one is a sand dollar, these are various odd shells, this is pink coral and here, last, but certainly not least, a couple of starfish. Do you like them?"

"They're lovely," Cassie breathed. "Did you find all these on the bottom of the ocean?"

"Sure! There's sheer beauty under that aqua water, sights that most people never see." Troy studied Cassie for a moment. "Hey, would you like to go out with me tomorrow?"

"Me? Oh, I don't know," she began somewhat uncertainly, not sure of what Steele would think about her going off with a stranger, a man whom she had just met in a most unorthodox manner. Or, on the other hand, would Steele even care?

"Say yes, Cassie. I know you would enjoy it. If you don't know how to snorkle, I'll teach you. It isn't difficult, not in the least, and we'll stay in shallow water." Troy's bright blue eyes pleaded silently with her. Then, "Whata ya say?" he urged.

"Well, why not?" Cassie blurted. She had meant to say it to herself but the words seemed to have tumbled out and before she could change her mind, Troy jumped to his feet, his young face beaming.

"Well, all right!" he exclaimed and Cassie didn't have the heart to let him down. "How about ten o'clock tomorrow morning? Is that okay with you?"

"That's fine. What do I bring?" she asked in turn.

"Just your own beautiful self, a bathing suit, and something to change into after diving. I'll bring a picnic lunch."

"Oh, but—"

"No 'buts,' Cassie. You'll be hungry and I want to do it. Settled?" Troy crooked a blond brow upward as he waited for her answer.

"Okay. Lunch, too." Cassie made to rise and Troy reached down, clasping her hands within his, and pulled her to her feet.

"Where do I pick you up, Cassie Layton?"

"Oh, I—I'd rather meet you," she stammered, bending to brush the sand from her clothes so that she could hide her telltale face from his gaze.

"Boyfriend?" Troy queried with interest. "Or is it a husband?"

"Neither!" Cassie set him straight on that score, then hastened to add, "It would just be better, that's all."

With a shrug of his broad shoulders, Troy conceded, "Okay, you know best. So where do we meet?"

"What about right here?"

"Right here it is, then," Troy agreed. "At ten o'clock tomorrow morning." He flicked the tip of Cassie's nose in a brotherly manner, reached down and retrieved his belongings. "You won't forget, will you?" he asked a bit anxiously.

"No, I won't forget," Cassie returned in amusement and, tossing a smile over her shoulder, she started up the beach toward the path leading to the condominium.

Steele was not at home when Cassie returned and she saw nothing of Helen Thorne as she made her way to the kitchen. There she found Letty whipping up a pineapple cake and mumbling to herself.

"Hi, Letty!" the girl called out cheerfully.

"And just where did you run off to?" the little old lady demanded. Her cheeks were flushed and one had a smudge of flour. A wisp of gray hair dangled on her forehead which she brushed at impatiently as she looked at Cassie accusingly and continued.

"Mr. Steele's out lookin' for you! He stalked out that door roarin', 'God only knows what she'll do or where she'll go.'" Letty had put a little drama in her voice, but now she implored earnestly, "Can you please tell me what's goin' on around here? It's for sure no one else will tell me!" She shook her head in confusion. "That Thorne woman spittin' like an alley cat . . . Mr. Steele cursin' and slammin' doors . . . I'll tell you, miss, it's enough to drive an old woman crazy!"

"Oh, Letty, you're precious!" Cassie's gay laughter filled the room and the old woman chuckled, in spite of herself. "You do go on so!" She shook a slim finger at the housekeeper. "And I have a feeling that you know much more than you're letting on!"

"You don't say!" Letty paused and Cassie watched the play of emotions on the woman's face followed by a smile as the old lady leaned forward to admit, "Well, if I *do,* and mind you, I'm not *sayin'* I do, it's because I do a little eavesdroppin' now and then. And I make good use of what I hear, young miss!"

"Do you, indeed!" Cassie pressed the advantage. "And what, may I ask, have you learned this day?" She tried hard to appear indifferent.

"Well, I learned that that Thorne woman thinks you're carryin' young Paul's child and that Mr. Steele isn't too sure about it either. Then you come along and put Miss Thorne in her place, real snappylike, but at the same time you put some doubts in my boy's mind as well. And in my own, I might add."

Letty waited for a denial, an admission, a reply of some kind, and when none was forthcoming, she pursued her own line of reasoning.

"Well, it's none of my business, of course, so I won't be askin' no questions. Like you said, it's nobody's business 'ceptin' your own." Letty turned to pour the cake batter into a pan, then set the empty bowl on the counter.

Cassie pulled the bowl forward and, settling herself on a high bar stool, began studiously to scrape the remains of the cake batter from the bowl.

Letty watched the girl covertly but did not venture to intrude on her thoughts. Instead, she busied herself with placing the cake pan into the oven and fussing about with pots and pans.

Finally Cassie reached a conclusion and, with a deep

sigh, she drew a ragged, uneven breath. Without looking at the older woman, she spoke slowly:

"Letty, I'm not pregnant. I am *not* carrying Paul's nor any other man's child. I haven't been feeling well, it's true. But it's because my emotions have been under a tremendous strain. I know that I'm not eating properly, I am not able to sleep more than a couple of hours at a time, I can't even think!"

She paused but Letty said nothing, just went about her chores as if she had not heard the confidences which Cassie was extending to her. However, the girl knew that Letty was listening with intense interest. She was a kind woman. Cassie was well aware of that fact and felt that perhaps the housekeeper would be able to help her understand what was happening to her. Besides, she realized gratefully, Letty was a good listener and it was nice to have someone to talk to. She decided to get it all out of her system.

"I met Paul some months ago in Miami. He was so sweet and attentive to me. He swept me off my feet, you might say. The result of it all was that I gave up my job, my apartment, my jewelry, my car—in short, I gave up everything I had to come here with him!" As if an afterthought, Cassie added hastily, "Well, not quite everything. I didn't give him my body! If I hadn't held out on that point he probably would have left me sooner than he did!"

"Young Paul has always been somewhat of a scoundrel, miss. I'm not sure just what it is that makes him do the things he does. I won't call it a wild streak, 'cause Mr. Steele has one of those and it don't make him do like young Paul." Letty stopped and shook her gray head. "That one sure is exasperatin'!"

"I—I thought I loved him," Cassie resumed her narrative. "And he said he loved me. He didn't, of course, only

I didn't know that at the time. I was blind . . . a fool! Why, I really believed everything he told me, Letty, even believed that he wanted to marry me! It wasn't until he walked out on me, the night Steele brought me here, that I learned the ugly truth!"

All the anger and hurt she had been feeling surged up within Cassie and her voice betrayed her profound bitterness.

Letty turned to the girl with a softness in her faded brown eyes and an understanding that could come only from someone who really cared. She reached out to stroke Cassie's honey brown hair with a gentle hand.

"You needn't say any more, child. I can see that it hurts you to talk about it."

"Oh, but I want to!" Cassie raised her tear-bright eyes beseechingly. "I *need* to talk about it. No one else knows, or cares, what I feel. But *you* do, Letty, don't you?" Her large brown eyes pleaded with the older woman, asking her to care.

"Of course I do, miss. And if you want to tell me all about it, then I'm here to listen," Letty assured quietly.

"It's all so confusing, so . . . so unreal! And I don't know where to turn or what to do!" Cassie cried desperately, a single tear coursing down her cheek.

"Are you in love with Mr. Steele, child?" Letty's question brought Cassie's head up with a start. "Isn't that what's got you so confused and so upset?"

"In love? With Steele?" The words were a mere whisper, then Cassie's voice strengthened as she blustered, "Whatever do you mean, Letty? I—I don't even *know* him! How can I love him?"

"You don't have to know someone long, Cassie, to fall in love with him."

Cassie was vaguely aware that the servant had called her "Cassie" for the first time since she had come here. Somehow it brought the two women closer, made it a woman-to-woman-level conversation rather than on a guest-servant relationship.

"No, you don't have to know them, at all," Letty was saying. "It's something that happens all the time. You see, child, no one ever purposely falls in love, it just happens. Mr. Steele is a good man and it wouldn't be hard to fall in love with him. He has a lot of love to give but he has yet to give it!"

Letty moved the mixing bowl aside and gripped both Cassie's hands within her own. "Listen to your heart, child. Don't try to fight what's there!"

"But is it really there, Letty? Is it love that's there?"

"Oh, indeed it is, miss! A love so strong that I saw it from the very beginning! It will be sweet and lasting, but only if you let it blossom into full bloom!"

"But Steele—Steele doesn't love me!" Cassie argued.

"Are you sure? Do you know his heart, his mind? You say you don't know the man, then how can you know his innermost feelings?" the old woman pointed out matter-of-factly.

With a broken intake of breath Cassie gently slipped her hands from the warm grasp of the other woman and, flinging outstretched arms on the counter, buried her head on them, groaning in perplexity and defeat.

"Why don't you go up to your room for a bit of rest, miss. I'll call you when dinner is ready," Letty told her kindly.

Cassie raised her head and looked at Letty with a tremulous smile. She was amazed at the wisdom and insight of the housekeeper. She felt relieved, as if she had shed a burden from her young shoulders, a load which had become too heavy for her to bear alone.

But was Letty right? Did Cassie love Steele? Had she really fallen in love and not even known it? It was true that she had felt all the desires, the passionate longings that she had never experienced with another man.

Seemingly oblivious of Letty's presence, Cassie stared out the window with unseeing eyes and silently appraised her emotions in the light of what the old woman had told her. Let's face it, my girl, she admonished herself, you allowed Steele Malone to take liberties that you never before allowed *anyone*. And you enjoyed it, were eager for the touch of his hands, his lips. You even felt empty and cheated after you had refused to accept the fulfillment you craved!

And in that moment Cassie came face to face with the truth! Yes, oh, yes! I *do* love Steele Malone! she admitted without reservation. The memory came to her unbidden of the first time she had looked up into his mysterious steel-gray eyes, and she realized that she had fallen in love with the tall, dark stranger as he towered above her on the deck of *Malone's Passion!*

"You're right, Letty—right about *everything!*" Cassie exclaimed as she rose from the bar stool and left the kitchen.

She made her way to her room for a well-needed rest, certain now of her own feelings. But the uncertainty of having Steele's love lay heavy on her heart.

7

~~~~~~~~~~~~~~

Cassie walked along the shore, her bare feet kicking the warm sand. The fine particles were caught by the wind and the bleached, tan dust settled before she kicked out at it again. She shaded her tawny eyes from the overhead sun as she peered down the stretch of beach.

A quick glance at her watch told her that the young man whom she had met yesterday would soon be arriving. Why had she said yes to his invitation? What would Steele think if he should see her with another man? Would it even matter to him? She guessed not. Steele had much more important things to think about—she was only a nuisance, someone for whom he felt responsible.

Letty had told her that Steele had returned home last evening after looking for her for a long time. "He was madder than a wet hen," the old woman had said, using one of her clichés, as she often did. "Why, he was headed up them stairs 'til I stopped him," Letty had laughed, then added, "Mr. Steele," I says, "you don't want to bother the child. She was so upset by you and that Thorne woman talkin' 'bout her like you did she just wanted to get away and I'd have done the same thing!"

Letty went on to tell Cassie that Steele had paused, looked up the stairs, run his fingers through his dark hair and, mumbling an oath under his breath, had said, "What am I going to do with her, Letty? I truly think I've bitten into a tempting, sweet apple and swallowed before I realized it was rotten!" Then he poured a drink, lit a cigarette, and paced the room like a caged animal.

Cassie had also learned that Steele had not eaten any dinner, had been a "real bear" and later had gone to the library. He had turned at the door and ordered that he was not to be disturbed unless the damned house was burning down!

"The man don't even know why he's so moody," Letty had voiced that morning at breakfast as Cassie had thoughtfully sipped her coffee. "He left the house this morning without so much as a word and without eating breakfast. Why, he didn't even have his morning cup of coffee!"

When Cassie had reported that she had heard Steele up until very late and had wanted to go downstairs and talk to him, to tell him the whole story of her involvement with Paul, Letty had listened and nodded her gray head in agreement that Cassie should have done just that. But Cassie had admitted to feeling cowardly about it, had been afraid that Steele wouldn't believe her, anyway, so she had stayed in her room.

"He's got a burr in his britches," Letty had chuckled, "and it's botherin' him plenty bad, I'd say! It'll bother him 'til he finds the thing and realizes what's causin' it, then he'll do somethin' about it!"

Well, Cassie was the "burr," the girl thought morosely, and it wasn't taking Steele long to realize that fact, and she was certain it wouldn't be long before he would "do somethin' about it." Something like sending her back to Miami and out of his life as soon as possible!

Cassie's heart lurched at the thought of never seeing him again, never again gazing into the gray depths of his haunting eyes, watching him move with catlike grace, hearing his velvety, deep voice or seeing the disarming, crooked smile lighting his handsome face.

Suddenly a shrill whistle brought Cassie back from her wandering thoughts with a start, and she turned to see Troy Warner walking toward her, a wicker basket tucked under his arm. She sighed wearily and placed a smile on her lips and waved to the young man. Maybe, just maybe, she could get through the day without further thoughts of Steele Malone, without the pain throbbing in her heart, without closing her eyes and immediately seeing his face.

Could she do it? Cassie asked herself. Well, maybe not, but she certainly intended to try!

And with a forced cheerfulness she shouted, "Hi, Troy!" and ran toward the handsome man.

"A real, honest-to-goodness ranch?"

"A real, honest-to-goodness ranch!" Troy confirmed, flicking the tip of Cassie's pert nose with a forefinger. "Even though it is the twentieth century there are still working ranches and plantations."

"I know that! It's just that I've never known anyone before who owned a ranch!" Her voice was filled with awe.

"Oh, I only own a small part of the WR. I have two older brothers."

"The 'WR?' " Cassie questioned with interest.

"Yes. The ranch is called the WR and has been for over a hundred years, now," Troy supplied as he took another bite of his corned beef sandwich and washed it down with cold beer. "You see, my great-grandfather Warner married a girl whose last name was Riley. The Rileys owned the adjoining spread and my great-grandmother inherited it. So they merged the two properties into one and it became the WR Ranch, derived from the Warner-Riley marriage."

"How very interesting!" Cassie removed the clear, clinging wrapper from her own sandwich and said thoughtfully, "You know, Troy, you don't talk like a real cowboy."

"And pray tell me, Miss Layton, just how does a 'real cowboy' talk?" he drawled mockingly.

"Well, they say things like 'howdy' . . . 'ma'am' . . . 'gitty up' . . . and 'whoa,'" Cassie teased playfully.

"I never say 'howdy.'" Troy stifled a threatening chuckle. "I do say 'ma'am' to my mother, and I admit to saying 'whoa' when I want my horse to stop."

Cassie had been unsure about meeting Troy that morning. She had reminded herself that she had just met him, and not in the conventional way at that. But he had seemed nice enough and she needed an outing. So what better way than to spend the day with someone like Troy Warner, she had argued with herself. After all, the man was handsome, easy to talk with, and he was about her own age. And, for some odd reason, she felt perfectly safe with him. He had seemed to want only friendship and hadn't come on to her like most men she had met.

Maybe she even needed a diversion, another man, to take her mind off Steele Malone. It could be that Letty was wrong after all, and that she herself could be mistaken in her own interpretation of her emotions. It was entirely possible that she had not fallen in love, but only thought she had.

If she found that she could be attracted to someone else, Cassie thought, then she couldn't be in love with

Steele. So she'd just give herself the chance, she had decided, and if Troy Warner showed an interest in her, then she would try to respond to that interest. If he attempted to kiss her, she would welcome that overture. To Cassie, this would be a way that she could know for sure about her feelings, her attraction for Steele.

But it had not worked out that way at all. Cassie had felt nothing but a friendly companionship with Troy and he had given absolutely no indication of any deep interest in her. Their day had been nothing more than a lighthearted rapport between friends.

Now here they sat on the beach, a blanket spread beneath them, as the cool breeze wafted in from the ocean and the day drew to an end. Their morning jaunt had been so enjoyable that it had lasted all day. All around them lay sun-kissed beach; palms swayed lazily and the sweet scent of tropical flowers assailed the air. The setting was romantic, the day had been perfect, but the man and woman didn't have romance in mind.

"Cassie, you're swell! I haven't had this much fun in a long time, not since—" Troy broke off abruptly.

Cassie's golden brown eyes studied Troy, noting an expression on his tanned handsome face that she recognized to be pain, and her heart went out to the young man beside her.

"Since what?" she asked softly.

Troy swallowed hard as he gazed out over the white-capped waves which rushed outward as soon as they washed in. There was a long silence before he replied in a choked voice:

"Not—not since Dee." He smiled sadly and turned to Cassie. With an outstretched hand he captured a wind-blown tress of her honey brown hair, winding it about his finger. "Her hair was the same tawny color as yours and she was sweet and gentle, like you!"

"Was? This 'Dee,' is she—Oh, Troy, is s—she dead?"

"No, Cassie, my Dee is not dead," he sighed deeply. "But it's a long story and I won't bore you with it."

"You wouldn't bore me," Cassie assured him quickly. "Troy, do you need someone to talk to?" She reached out and laid her hand on his arm, her voice low. "I'm here, if you do."

"Are you sure you don't mind listening?" he asked anxiously.

"Very sure!"

"I met Dee last year on a buying trip to Arizona when my oldest brother and I had gone there to look over some cattle. You see, each year they have state rodeos and livestock shows. We had a meeting with this guy to see two of his prize bulls and when we went into the holding barn, there was this little slip of a girl struggling with a saddle twice her size." Troy chuckled at the memory before continuing.

"It was love at first sight." His blue eyes held Cassie. "You may not believe in such a thing."

"Oh, I believe in it, all right," she whispered, remembering the first time she had seen Steele, how her heart had raced out of control and she hadn't been able to speak. Yes, it had been love at first sight for Cassie, only it had taken a long time for her to admit it.

"The problem was that Dee was only sixteen," Troy was saying. "I tried to stay away from Dee, I really did, but I couldn't! There was something about her—" Troy paused as if searching for his next words. "Then one night the situation just got out of hand and the next thing . . . Cassie, I made love to her, I made her mine.

"After I returned to my home in Colorado I knew that I had to see her again. I began making frequent 'business trips' back to Arizona on the pretext that I was looking for cattle. Of course I saw Dee each time and eventually I

100

learned that she was pregnant with my child. We decided to run away and get married, but her father caught us. Dee told him that she loved me and was going to have my baby, thinking he would allow us to be married. But it didn't work out that way. Instead, he sent Dee off to her mother somewhere in Ohio and beat me unmercifully. But I wouldn't fight back because he was Dee's father and a lot older man than me. He ordered me to stay away and added that he'd kill me if I ever tried to see Dee again!"

"How terrible for you! You—you mean you don't know where she is? And you don't know how to find her?" Cassie asked in dismay.

By a weak shake of his blond head Troy confirmed that he didn't know.

"I'm so sorry, Troy! I wish I could help! I wish that there was some way . . ." Cassie's words trailed away and her warm eyes glistened with unshed tears. Impulsively she reached out, her arms encircled Troy's neck, and she held him close. "You'll find Dee again, I *know* you will," Cassie cried softly into his shoulder. "You'll find her!"

The two sat thus for several moments in companionable silence. Each knew that he had found a friend in the other and the care and understanding that they both needed. Cassie wanted to help, to comfort Troy. He had been hurt, had felt pain and longing even as she had.

"Thanks for listening, Cassie. I've never told this to anyone else and it has helped me to talk about it." Troy seemed grateful for her sympathetic understanding.

Cassie's arms tightened about him in a swift, reassuring hug and Troy dropped a light kiss on her brow as they sat quietly watching the golden sun slip slowly from the multicolored sky to settle into the arms of the blue velvet waters.

And neither was aware of the tall man standing beyond them on the ridge, his fists clenched at his sides, his black hair blowing in the evening breeze and a storm brewing in his smoky gray eyes.

The atmosphere was charged with hostility and a nerve-racking silence claimed the room. There was a distinct wariness hovering over the occupants seated at the large dining table.

Helen Thorne sat at one end of the long table, an empty dinner plate before her, as she made use of the white wine. The woman downed one glass after the other as her dark green eyes shot daggers from Cassie to Steele and back again. Her crimson mouth was compressed in a thin, cruel line and her high cheekbones were splotched with angry color.

Steele ate with quiet control, almost mechanically, but it seemed to Cassie that it was taking quite an effort for him to suppress his apparent anger. His tanned fingers tightened about the stem of his crystal wine glass as he lifted it to his lips, and the muscles in his jaw worked spasmodically even when he was not eating.

Cassie, unsure of what may have transpired between the two before she had returned that evening, sat in discomfiture not daring to break the silence that held the room in its grip.

Her appetite definitely affected by the tension, not to mention her late lunch with Troy, Cassie toyed with her food, pushing it about her plate with her fork. Twice she managed to meet Steele's gaze but both times her body actually shuddered at the malevolence in the gray depths of his eyes.

Even Letty seemed unusually subdued. The kindly old woman entered the room only once during the interminable meal, and that was to bring a newly filled decanter of wine. Letty had said nothing, her face inscrutable, stealing one quick glance at Cassie before hastily retreating.

What in thunder is going on, Cassie wondered. Has something happened? And if so, had it anything to do with her? Well, she decided, she wouldn't sit here another moment in this stormy atmosphere and, carefully placing her fork on the table, she removed her napkin from her lap.

"If you two will excuse me?" Cassie said quietly as she started to rise.

"Aren't you hungry, Cassie?" Steele asked. His low, dangerous tone made her spine prickle uncomfortably.

"Ah—well, not really, I guess," she stammered, feeling most uneasy.

"Finish your dinner, Cassie!" There was no doubt that it was a command.

Cassie's eyes met Steele's in a flash, an angry red fired her cheeks.

"I'm a grown woman, Steele Malone, and I'll not be ordered about!" she snapped in her own defense. She shoved her chair back and sprang to her feet, toppling the chair behind her. Steele Malone, with his—his damned arrogance and his demands, treating her as if she were a three year old, telling her "finish your dinner, Cassie!" The nerve of him, she fumed. The very nerve!

Cassie turned to stalk from the room but had gone no further than a few steps before she was seized with an iron grip and jerked backward, off balance.

Staring up into the deep gray of Steele's eyes, Cassie found it hard to breathe and hard to think. Her heart was beating rapidly and her breath came in short gasps. When Steele's grip tightened on her arm, she had to fight back the tears swimming beneath her lids.

Cassie struggled briefly to free herself but to no avail. Anger flared through her as she realized she was completely helpless in Steele's grasp and that Helen Thorne was looking on in smug amusement. That fact provided her with an outlet for her dilemma and she blazed at Steele.

"Why don't you exert your strong-arm tactics on Helen? She hasn't eaten any dinner either. All she has succeeded in doing is to diminish your liquor supply!"

"Helen is not my responsibility!" Steele rasped.

Lifting her glass high in a drunken salute, Helen mocked, "That's right, 'little one!'" She lowered the glass to her lips and gulped the contents, then reached for the decanter. "Mr. Malone has tired of me and wants to move on to greener, and I might add, younger, pastures. He wants y—"

"Shut up, Helen!" Steele broke in, his anger getting out of control.

"No! Let her finish, Steele!" Cassie demanded as the man loosened his grip on her arm. Then, to Helen, "He wants what?"

Cassie saw the other woman look furtively at Steele and noted the threat in the glare of his gray eyes which had darkened to near-black with the depth of his unspoken warning. Both women knew that it was not an idle threat which the angry man issued.

Helen shrugged a shapely shoulder and replied, "He wants to know why you didn't invite your young, handsome, blond beachboy!" She laughed shrilly, a brittle sound in the suddenly still room.

Cassie froze. So Steele had seen her with Troy! Was that why he had been so angry? Could that conceivably be the reason for his silence? What was he thinking, she wondered and, turning toward Steele, she watched the changing emotions cross his face. Dear God! He looked ready to explode!

"What are you talking about?" Cassie asked, avoiding Steele's piercing dark gaze. "I don't know what you mean!"

"Not only does Cassie have a nasty temper, darling, she is also a liar!" Helen purred thickly as she rose from her chair. She stood, swaying slightly, then made her unsteady way toward the living room. Stopping in the doorway, she clutched at the frame and tossed over her shoulder, "I wouldn't make him any angrier, my dear child. Steele has an awfully foul temper when he's riled!"

Cassie watched as Helen disappeared into the next room. She wanted to run, to hide. Her body trembled in fearful anticipation. What would Steele do, she thought frantically. What *could* he do? After all, it was her own life. He had no claim on her, none whatsoever. He had absolutely no right to question—

"I am normally a patient man, Cassie, but I *will* not be lied to!" Steele's words were clipped and his broad chest heaved as he crossed his arms over it.

"But—"

"Don't!" The one word seemed to reach out and slap Cassie. "I was walking on the beach and I saw the two of you!" Steele turned away with a groan, running his hands through his hair. "There you were with your arms around him. And he kissed you, Cassie," he spun around and stared accusingly at her. "I saw him kiss you!"

"All right! All *right!*" Cassie shouted, fanning the air with outspread hands. "So you saw us! What's the big deal?"

With a tremendous effort Steele regained his composure and assumed indifference. "It's really nothing to me. But what about my brother?"

"Paul?" Cassie asked, bewildered.

"I have only one brother!" Steele replied coldly.

"This has nothing to do with Paul, nor with you! Troy and—"

"*Troy!* So you're on a first-name basis, are you?" Steele thundered.

Tossing her head, Cassie answered candidly, "Well,

you would expect that, would you not, when you saw us wrapped in each other's arms!"

The shot hit home but Steele chose to ignore it and asked instead, "How long have you known this 'Troy,' Cassie?" Without waiting for an answer to that question, he fired a couple more. "Where did you meet him? Is he your new lover?"

The demanding questions both embarrassed and infuriated Cassie. She stepped close to Steele and, through clenched teeth, hissed in his face, "That is none of your damned business!"

"Well, I'm *making* it my 'damned business!'" Steele informed her. His long fingers gripped both her wrists and he jerked Cassie forward against his solid chest. "You told me that Paul still held your heart. That was your reason for holding out on me that night. You allowed my caresses up to a point, then you restrained me from the fulfillment we both desired! Was it really because of Troy, rather than for Paul's sake? Tell me, Cassie, is Troy your new lover?"

Suddenly weary of the whole thing, Cassie returned dispiritedly, "I only met Troy yesterday. It would be rather soon to tumble into bed with him, Steele."

"*Time* has little to do with desire, Cassie." Steele's hands released her wrists to travel slowly up her bare arms, coming to rest on her shoulders. He held Cassie from him while his gray gaze roamed over her. "You are a beautiful woman, Cassie. And a passionate one!" he murmured, his voice husky. "And you have a body— God! A body that cries out to be touched!"

Cassie felt her immediate response. A tingling sensation swept over her entire body and the blood coursed hotly through her veins. There it is, again, she thought in wonder, that current which flowed so strongly between the two of them. She had admitted to herself and to Letty that she was in love with Steele, but what was it that drew him to her like a moth to a flame?

His reaction to her relationship with Troy smacked of jealousy, yet Steele had never given her reason to think he felt any emotion other than desire and passion. So why should it matter to him if Troy was her lover?

Cassie shook her head in confusion and Steele, mistaking the negative movement, drew her close against his hard frame with one arm about her shoulder, the fingers of his other hand playing along her back, feeling the taut muscles relax under his touch.

"Please!" Cassie whispered.

"What is it you want? What are you longing for?"

"I—I don't know what it is that I—" She broke off and, again shaking her head, sighed raggedly. "I just don't know!"

Steele's smoky gray eyes held hers, burning desire mirrored in them.

"I know what you want, Cassie."

Steele's dark head descended, his warm breath mingling with her own. A soft moan escaped Cassie just before Steele's lips claimed hers in a passionate kiss which seemed to draw every ounce of resistance from her.

Cassie's supple body molded to the muscular contour of Steele's rock-hard frame, and her arms lifted of their own accord to find their way about his neck. Her fingers entwined themselves deep into the thickness of his black mane.

Just as Cassie felt herself begin to drift away on a cloud of complete surrender, eagerly responding to Steele's kiss, she heard a groan emerge from him and a shudder claim his body. Time seemed to stand still and Steele and Cassie were oblivious to the fact that they were still standing in the dining room.

Suddenly a high-pitched cackle of laughter invaded their consciousness. Cassie started guiltily but Steele only lifted his head, still holding her to him. They both stared toward the doorway leading to the living room.

Helen Thorne stood clapping her hands slowly as she sang out, "Bravo! Oh, bravo! Such an interesting performance, my dears!"

It was mid-morning of the next day before Cassie made an appearance. She had slept badly, as usual, and her sleep had been invaded by dreams of the events of the preceding evening. During her waking hours she had relived the scenes as they had actually happened. She could still feel Steele's strong arms about her and her lips burned from his arousing kisses.

At the time of Cassie and Steele's passionate embrace, not once had it entered Cassie's head that Letty could walk in on them at any minute. She had thought Helen Thorne to be too far gone to make another entrance. Now she felt her body grow hot with embarrassment that Helen had witnessed her wanton conduct. How could I have let myself get carried away like that, she fumed.

Cassie retrieved a pitcher of tomato juice from the refrigerator and poured the chilled red liquid into a small glass. She sank wearily to a bar stool and set the glass of juice on the counter, one long, slender finger tracing the droplets of frost which formed on the glass from the cold contents.

Her head was aching and Cassie massaged the muscles in the back of her neck. She couldn't face Helen today, Cassie thought with a groan, nor Steele either! She was sure that Helen would make some ugly comment about last night. The woman was the kind of person who thrived on making people feel uncomfortable, especially someone she didn't like, and right now Cassie felt that she headed Helen's list! She had never felt anything but hostile dislike from the first time she had met the woman. From the beginning Cassie had known that Helen considered her an enemy and nothing during their acquaintance had given her reason to feel otherwise.

A sound from the side door turned Cassie's attention in that direction and she watched as Letty came into the kitchen, struggling with a large wicker basket filled with folded laundry.

"Hi, Letty!" Cassie greeted her with a disarming smile.

"Hello, missy, and how are you this fine day?" The housekeeper made her way to the counter with her burden. Lifting the basket, she placed it upon one of the tall bar stools.

"I'm fine, I think," Cassie answered Letty's question before taking a sip of her juice. "Though I didn't rest well again last night."

"And who in this house *did*? What with all the shoutin' and cussin'," the woman complained.

Cassie made no comment and busied herself with pouring another glass of juice. "Oh?" was all that Cassie had to say to encourage the woman to proceed with the information the girl wanted.

"That Thorne woman sure got what she was askin' for!" Letty stated with satisfaction. She laughed shortly and shook her gray head. "She pushed just too far, I'd say. I've been waitin' for her to do it and last night was the last straw!"

"But what happened, Letty?"

"Well, the real excitement was shortly after the—ah— well, after Miss Thorne walked in and saw Mr. Steele kissin' you. I would say that Helen Thorne got a mite hot under the collar when she witnessed that little episode."

Letty had the grace to flush and Cassie realized that the housekeeper had no doubt been watching from the kitchen and that she, too, had "witnessed that little episode."

After a brief silence, Letty continued.

"Miss Thorne flew into a rage and accused Mr. Steele of lots of things. She cursed a lot, very unladylike, I must say, and she called you lots of names, missy. That's when Mr. Steele was pushed too far and he interrupted her and said, 'You'll not speak like that of Cassie, Helen, not in my presence nor in my house.' Then she screamed at him, 'You want your brother's mistress. You want that b—.' That's when Mr. Steele told her, 'Get upstairs and get packed! I want you out of my house tonight and out of my life forever!' "

Cassie could only listen in amazement and wished she had stayed for that confrontation instead of fleeing to her room. But Letty hadn't finished with her dramatic account of last night's happenings.

"Mr. Steele called a taxi and ordered them to be no more than ten minutes and when Miss Thorne heard that, she went upstairs and threw all her things into her bags and brought them downstairs herself. Mr. Steele didn't even help her!

"After she left, Mr. Steele downed two scotch and waters, grabbed his coat and yelled at me. 'Letty!' he says, 'don't look for me 'til late tomorrow!' Then he banged the door shut behind him and I haven't seen the boy nor heard from him since!"

Letty finished her long narrative with a heavy sigh.

After a time, Cassie rose from the bar stool and walked wordlessly to the front door, closing it carefully behind her. She felt the need to be alone with her thoughts, as she had done once before, and headed for the deserted beach where she could sort out the details of the events Letty had described.

Why would Steele kick out his own mistress in defense of Cassie, whom he believed to be his brother's mistress? It just didn't make any sense to her and she shook her head in confusion and frustration.

There was no doubt in Cassie's mind that Helen
Thorne had been Steele's mistress. Hadn't she heard
Helen's laughter and Steele's deep voice in the bedroom
next to hers on the morning after she had arrived here?
Had she not seen Steele emerge from the bathroom
adjoining that room in a state of undress? Had she not
seen Helen's filmy, black negligee tossed across the
rumpled bed in that same room? Even now another
memory came to Cassie's mind. Letty's words, "Mr.
Steele and her was to be married once."

So what had happened, Cassie wondered? What had
gone wrong? And dear God! Why did she have to
become involved? More important, why did she fall in
love with Steele Malone!

Her mind filled with unanswered questions and her
heart full of conflicting emotions, Cassie plodded along
the beach with her head bent, for one time completely
unmindful of the beauty of the island.

8

~~~~~~~~~~~

Cassie had walked for a long time, sorting out all the things which were so perplexing to her, and when she turned to retrace her steps back to Steele's penthouse she felt much relieved. She had reached the conclusion that she must leave Nassau, that it was time for her to get away from Steele and attempt to forget the man and her love for him.

She would ask Troy's help, she decided. Troy was leaving the island in the morning to return home and they had agreed to meet late this afternoon at their usual spot, just to say good-bye. At that time she could enlist his help. It would mean that she'd have to tell him the story behind it all, but they were friends and she felt that he would understand.

After all, she had shared Troy's personal heartache, Cassie reminded herself, and had given him her understanding and felt that he had drawn much strength from that sharing. There was no doubt in her mind that he would help her in any way he possibly could and there was no one else here she could go to. Not here, nor anywhere else, Cassie told herself truthfully.

This was the first time she had ever felt so completely alone since both her parents had been killed, leaving her with no known relatives. There had always been just the three of them, very close, very loving, and suddenly there was only Cassie, who had been fortunate that it happened after she had finished school. Although young, she had managed to get by on the small nest egg they had left her. There was not a vestige of that money left but Cassie had worked steadily, making a fairly comfortable living until she had met Paul Malone.

Cassie did not choose to dwell on that subject because it made her feel an utter fool to have been taken in so completely by the scoundrel. He had taken from her all her belongings with the exception of her clothes and the seventy-five dollars which she had guiltily tucked away in the bottom of her bag.

The same seventy-five dollars which she had offered to Steele that first night to help pay her way back to Miami. He had refused the money and later Cassie had found the crumpled bills stuffed in her purse. The last time she had remembered seeing the money was when she had thrust it at Steele and he had not accepted it, leaving the money to fall heedlessly to the cabin floor of his boat. She had been surprised, she recalled, when she had found it since she had not been aware that he had recovered the scattered bills.

Well, seventy-five dollars would buy her plane fare back to Miami, but what would she do when she got back, Cassie thought in dismay. She would have no place to stay until she could find a job. The solution would be to ask her friend Troy for a loan until she could again become able to meet her financial obligations.

Cassie reached this decision and the kitchen at the

same time and called out to Letty. There was no answer and she crossed to the refrigerator for a glass of cold milk, but as she reached for the handle her eyes rested upon a note attached to the refrigerator door by a bright yellow daisy magnet.

Letty had gone to the market, the note read, and should be back within the hour. She had left a bowl of fresh chicken salad, Letty had written and had added beneath her signature, "Mr. Steele phoned to say he would be home in time for dinner."

At that information Cassie felt her heart lurch, then begin to pound. She didn't want ever to leave Steele but she knew she must. For her own good, even for her sanity! After tonight, Cassie hoped to be on her way back home, no longer to be dependent upon the generosity of Steele Malone.

Cassie made a chicken salad sandwich, sliced a tomato on a bed of crisp lettuce, and topped it off with two spoonfuls of cottage cheese. Then she poured the glass of cold milk she had wanted and placed her light meal on a serving tray to transport it to the library. She could think of no place she'd rather sit for a while. That room seemed so full of Steele's presence that she wanted to spend this time alone there. It would be the last time, she thought, and she could take the memory with her.

"Letty, I'll be out for a while," Cassie told the house-keeper softly.

"Oh? And will you be back in time for dinner?" Letty asked.

"Yes, I'm sure that I will," Cassie replied as she pulled a light woolen shawl about her shoulders and started toward the living room only to be stopped by Letty's questioning.

"Are you going to meet that young man, miss?" the woman inquired stiffly.

"Yes." Cassie's answer was brief, and she noted the disapproving expression on Letty's face.

"Miss, do you think that's a good idea? Mr. Steele's been quite upset over you seeing that man."

"But I'm only going to say good-bye, Letty. Troy is leaving for home in the morning. Besides, he is my friend!" Cassie said as an afterthought. She didn't want Letty to know that she was planning to leave. She liked the older woman and would miss her. Also, she was sure that Letty would tell Steele that she was planning to leave and Cassie didn't want that to happen. Somehow she felt that if Steele knew of her plans he'd try to stop her.

Pausing in the doorway, Cassie implored, "Letty, please don't tell Steele where I've gone!"

The housekeeper merely nodded her head in acknowledgment of Cassie's request.

Afternoon was coming to an end and a cool breeze drifted across the ocean. Dusk had become the most favorite time for Cassie on this beautiful island. As the sun mingled with the sea and disappeared, leaving the red-orange glow to settle over the land, Cassie stared out over the water wondering if any happiness waited for her out there somewhere. But she knew in her heart that if Steele was not in her life she would never be truly happy.

Nearing their designated meeting place, Cassie scanned the beach, her big brown eyes searching for Troy. The stretch of beach was deserted and she wondered if perhaps she might be late, but a glance at her watch showed her that she was right on time. Maybe Troy was going to be late, though in the brief time she had known him he had never been late.

Cassie wandered on down the beach to wait for Troy, and as she reached a massive piece of driftwood her gaze was drawn to an object glowing in the late afternoon light. It was a pink pearled conch shell about the size of her hand and beautifully cleaned and polished. Reaching down, Cassie picked up the shell to investigate and there, nestled inside, was a folded sheet of paper.

Curious, Cassie removed the paper and, unfolding it, read the note which had been scrawled in a bold masculine handwriting.

> *Dear, beautiful Cassie:*
>
> *Since I'll not be here in person, since I could not leave without saying good-bye, this note will have to say the words which I cannot.*
>
> *I met your Mr. Malone and he told me nicely, yet firmly, that I was never to see you again. I think he misunderstood our relationship and he didn't give me a chance to explain.*
>
> *Cassie, you are one of the most giving and understanding friends I have ever had. I will miss you and never will I forget you! If ever you are in the Denver area, please let me hear from you.*
>
> *After our talk and your belief that I would one day find Dee, I have decided to look for her and have made up my mind that I will find her if I have to search for the rest of my life!*
>
> *I trust that you will find that for which you are seeking and that you, my dear friend, will be happy.*
>
> *Troy*

So Steele had told Troy to stay away from her! And that's why he had not come to meet her as planned! How *dare* Steele Malone do such a thing! He had no right!

Cassie was furious that Steele would presume to order Troy to do anything. Troy Warner was his own man and she, Cassie, was her own person and not Steele's property, as he seemed to be treating her!

Then she remembered that she had come here for a dual purpose. Not only had she come to say good-bye to Troy but to ask his assistance in the form of a loan to see her through the next few weeks. Now Steele had destroyed her last chance, her last hope of escaping. In effect, she was back at square one!

Well, he would certainly hear about this, she fumed. Mr. Malone would have *her* to answer to for his meddling and for his presumptuousness. Just who did he think he was, anyhow? What right had he to tell a man to leave her alone as if he owned her?

Cassie stormed back up the beach. Her face was flushed with anger and her fists were clenched in a threatening manner. The man was insufferable! He was an overbearing, domineering, pompous jackass and she was going to tell him that, along with a few other choice things! Oh, but she'd make him sorry he'd ever met her, Cassie swore!

All these thoughts were sweeping through her mind as Cassie entered the elevator and jabbed angrily at the button indicating the fourteenth floor.

"Damn!" she swore hotly as she realized she had broken a fingernail. "You'll pay for that, too, Steele Malone!" Cassie declared loudly in the empty elevator car.

To her great disappointment Steele had not yet returned and it further infuriated her. She wanted to confront him while she was at the height of her anger. But only Letty sat at the kitchen counter, her gray head resting on her outstretched arms.

"Where is Steele?" Cassie demanded.

Letty's head came up with a start and the old woman focused her eyes on the girl standing before her.

"He hasn't come home yet, missy," the housekeeper answered slowly, studying the anger on the lovely young face. "Has something upset you, child? Are you angry about something?"

"Angry? Am I angry?" Cassie exploded. "Oh, Letty, if I could get my hands around Steele Malone's neck I'd strangle him with my bare hands! I'd—I'd kill him! Why, I'd—"

"Whoa! Settle down, missy. Just what has Mr. Steele done to get you so riled up?" the older woman wanted to know.

"He's involved himself with my life, that's what he's done!" Cassie cried in pure frustration as she paced the floor. "He's made me feel things I don't want to feel! He's—he's arrogant and domineering and conceited and lordly and—and—"

"Cocky?" Letty supplied in amusement.

"Yes!"

"And don't forget 'dictatorial.' "

"Right!"

"Not to mention 'presumptuous.' "

"You've got it!"

"And 'vain'?"

"That, too!"

"Is that enough names to call Mr. Steele?" Letty asked.

"Not nearly!" the irate Cassie returned.

"Well, I suppose that'll have to do, since we've both about exhausted the ones we know," the housekeeper told Cassie with a lighthearted chuckle. "Now, would you like to tell me what has happened? What's turned a sweet, young child like you into a ravin' spitfire?"

"Steele Malone! *That's* what's happened! He had no right! None at all!" Cassie began, stamping her foot in anger. She proceeded to tell Letty about Troy, their meeting and subsequent friendship, and what Steele had done. How he had told Troy to "leave be, hands off," Cassie voiced in her own words.

She went on to tell Letty about finding the beautiful conch shell and the note which had been tucked inside, after which Cassie thrust the shell into Letty's hands and unfolded the note to read it aloud.

When she finished reading, Cassie sank dejectedly to a bar stool and with a deep sigh asked, *"Why,* Letty? Why would Steele do such a thing? He had absolutely no right!"

But Letty had no reply, only shook her graying head to indicate that she had no answers for Cassie's questions and no defense for Steele's actions.

The sudden ring of the telephone prevented any further discussion between the two women and Letty rose to answer the summons, placing the pink shell on the counter before Cassie.

But the distraught girl, simmering with her anger and frustration, paid no heed to the beautiful object nor to Letty's conversation on the telephone.

"That was Mr. Steele," the housekeeper volunteered as she returned to Cassie's side. "He won't be home for dinner, after all. And he said that he may not make it back home until tomorrow, he's trying to get a plane out of Miami, now."

"Miami?" The single word shot from the girl's mouth.

"Yes, miss, that's what he said."

"But why didn't he take me with him if he was going to Miami? He was supposed to get me back there, that was our agreement! The only reason I'm still here is because we couldn't sail in that terrible storm. He never suggested that we could go any other way! So why would he go back there without making arrangements to take me with him?" Cassie shook her head in perplexity.

"I'm sure he had his reasons, child," the kindly Letty soothed.

"His reasons! *His!* What about *me?* What about *my* reasons for wanting to leave here, Letty? I've been tied to

Steele Malone for far too long! I can't think for myself—God! I can't even breathe! He's taken over my entire life, Letty! He acts as if he owns me!"

"Do you really want to leave Nassau that badly, child?"

"Of course I do! Don't you see, Letty, I *have* to!" Cassie stated simply.

"But what will you do there? What's there for you?"

"Oh, I don't know, and at this point I don't even care!"

"Then try to be content to stay right here. You're wanted in this house and besides, Mr. St—" The woman's words broke off abruptly and she turned to the stove, busying herself with dinner preparations. "This stew will be ready shortly, miss."

"What about Mr. Steele? What were you about to say? What do you know?" the suspicious young woman demanded.

Letty stood for a moment without turning, then took a deep breath but made no reply. Cassie felt that the woman was hiding something or knew something which she was uncertain whether or not to disclose.

"Letty?" she prompted softly.

As if making a sudden decision, the housekeeper turned to Cassie, wiping work-worn, shaking hands on her apron.

"Mr. Steele won't let you go, miss. Even if you managed to get back home he'd come after you. He'd never allow you to stay, he'd—he'd bring you back!"

Cassie stared at Letty, her tawny brown eyes uncomprehending and bewildered.

"Wouldn't allow? Why, Steele couldn't stop me! He wouldn't even know where I was!" she answered in a shocked voice. "The man must be insane!" she added with a nervous laugh.

"Maybe so, but he means what he says!"

"He told you this? All that you've just told me?"

"Yes, miss," Letty replied in a mere whisper. Then she swallowed hard, as if she were trying to free something lodged in her throat.

"Is there something else? You may as well tell me everything!" Cassie told her bluntly.

"Well, miss, I've never seen him so furious as he was the night when he came back to the house after he'd seen you with that young man on the beach," the old woman began. "He was—well, he was like a madman! He swore and slammed into the library and I heard him on the telephone. I didn't hear everything, but I did hear him say, 'I won't stand for it! I'll not let her go back to that kind of life!' His voice was so cold, miss, it made me shudder. I didn't ask him no questions and I didn't make any comments, but I am sure that Mr. Steele is concerned about you and the kind of life he *thinks* you'd been leadin'. And the more I think about it . . . I'm sure there's much more to his anger than I'm aware of . . . or, maybe, than *he's* aware of!" The last words were thoughtful.

Cassie had listened intently without interruption, though questions kept coming to her mind. She decided she might learn more by listening than by questioning. But what could she say? She didn't understand any of what Letty had said. None of it made sense. Why should it matter to Steele what I do . . . where I go . . . what kind of life I lead? Cassie was thinking. Her head was spinning with the effort of trying to sort out this new information, none of which made the least bit of sense.

Perhaps she should leave now, before Steele returned, Cassie thought. He was in Miami, that much she knew for sure, so she should be able to get away without his or Letty's knowledge or interference.

The important thing was to get back home, and she would take one thing at a time once she got there. Susie, the girl in the apartment next to hers, would probably let Cassie bunk with her for a few days, at least until she had found a job. And when she told Mrs. McKay all that had happened, there was a possibility that her supervisor would be understanding enough to give her job back to her. They had not found a replacement for her before she left, so just maybe . . . She realized that she was grasping at straws, but Cassie knew one thing for certain—she had to get away tonight!

Rising slowly from the bar stool, her face pale and puzzled, Cassie did not hear Letty's words of compassion and the old woman called to her again.

"Are you all right, missy?"

"Uh—yes, I'm okay."

"Are you sure? And where are you going?" this last due to Cassie's heading toward the stairway.

"I'm going to pack my bags, Letty," she informed her inquisitor. "I'm—I'm leaving here before Steele gets back. Once I'm gone he won't have to worry about me or my life! And he won't know where to find me!"

"He'll know, child," Letty stated quietly but firmly. "Mr. Steele has known your every move for days. That phone call he made, it was to that private investigator Mr. Steele hired to—"

"No!" Cassie was aghast. "Oh, Letty, are you sure? But—but why? Tell me *why?*" She was verging on hysteria.

"He thinks you'll go back to young Paul, miss. Or go away with Mr. Warner," Letty told her matter-of-factly. "And he's determined that it doesn't happen!"

Cassie only stared at the woman. She felt like a prisoner! Had Steele Malone become her jailer? This was all so unreal, so unbelievably incredible!

"He's a strong man, miss," Letty was saying. "And powerful! You can't fight him, there's no use to try. Mr. Steele will have his way—he always does!"

9

~oecccccecsea~

Cassie stood before the open window of her room, staring unseeingly out into the moonlit night. She clutched the blue gossamer curtains in her small hands as if for support and tears trickled slowly down her flushed cheeks. An uncontrollable tremor claimed her body and she pressed her brow against the cool window frame.

So lost was she in her thoughts and inner turmoil that Cassie didn't hear the muffled knock at her door, nor did she hear the door open. Only when the ghostly shadow fell across the room did she jump and turn toward the source.

Her gaze met the tall form of Steele standing in the middle of her dimly lit room. He stood with feet braced apart, his hands thrust deep into the pockets of his tight-fitting jeans and his shirt unbuttoned, with the shirt tail hanging loosely about his slim hips.

He looked so handsome, Cassie thought fleetingly, even sexy in his state of dishevelment, and all the fight seemed to go out of her. She felt all the hate and frustration draining away.

No! she shook herself mentally. No! He won't do this to me! She'd face Steele with her anger, she thought fiercely, and tell him what she thought of him and his high-handed ways, his interference in her life!

"How dare you!" Cassie spat at him, anger surging anew. She made a slow approach toward Steele. "How dare you interfere in my life! You have no claim on me and there's no justification for what you've done! You can't tell Troy Warner or any other man to stay away from me! You don't own me, Steele Malone, and you never will!"

Steele hadn't moved or spoken during her outburst and in the duskiness Cassie could see the rise and fall of his broad chest as it heaved threateningly. His breath sounded loud in the sudden silence of the room.

Was he going to say anything, she wondered uneasily as a slight chill seemingly filled the air. Cassie didn't know what to say or do. His behavior mystified her and she actually wondered if it were really Steele Malone who was standing there in the shadows, taking the brunt of her fury so unflinchingly. Could it be possible that he believed her to be justified in her anger?

Just as the silence became unbearable, Steele spoke in a low, silky tone.

"I thought that by now, Cassie, you would know me well enough to understand that when I want something, I'll have it! I wanted Warner out of your life and—well, I've seen to it that he is! I want my brother out of your life, as well, and I will see to it that he is!

"Furthermore, if any other man attempts to enter your life and, with his silvery tongue, smooth talk his way into your bed, then he, too, will have me to deal with! I give you fair warning!"

"How dare you!" Cassie screamed in cold rage and

she struck out at him, only to have Steele grasp her wrists in a painful grip.

"I dare anything I damn well please!" he bit out dangerously as his gray eyes glittered in the dimness. "I want you, Cassie Layton, and I'll not share you with any man!"

Cassie was taken aback. He *wanted* her?

Steele held her in his iron grip, his body rigid with purpose, his breath hot against her brow. "My brother's a fool, a real fool! He has never lived up to his responsibilities, never! Not only is Paul a fool, but he's weak. Do you want a man that isn't a real man?"

Cassie stood uncertainly in Steele's powerful grip, not sure whether to risk increasing his rage by attempting to justify herself. She had no chance to reply, however, because Steele was ranting on.

"Paul's wife will never give him a divorce, he'll never be free for you! He won't be free to give your child a name!" he rasped, shaking Cassie as if she were a rag doll. Then Steele's grip loosened about Cassie's smarting wrists and he set her from him. He walked to the window and, seating himself on the ledge, ran his fingers along the back of his neck as he stared out into the night.

After a lengthy silence, during which Cassie dared not speak, Steele's voice came to her in low, vibrant tones.

"Cassie, I've done a lot of thinking about this . . . hell, I've done too much thinking . . . now it's time to do something! There is only one solution to this situation and I've already made the arrangements." Steele paused and took a deep breath before he continued. "Your only choice is to marry me!"

"Marry you?" Cassie repeated the words, not absolutely sure she had heard correctly. Marry Steele? In God's name, *why?* He didn't love her and he didn't know that she was in love with him, so was the man crazy?

"Marry you?" she reiterated. "Have you lost your mind?"

Cassie whirled to meet the level gaze of Steele's dark gray eyes. When she saw that he was serious, a bubble of laughter welled within her and, making its way upward, burst from her lips.

"I wouldn't marry you, Steele Malone, if you were the last man on earth! Why, I—I don't even *like* you! I'm trying to get *away* from you, for heaven's sake! I certainly don't want to be tied to you for the rest of my life!"

Steele sat at the window making no move while Cassie threw the words at him. The only indication that her blunt words had made any impression on him was the clenching of his fists. Then he spoke slowly and deliberately.

"The way I see it, Cassie, you have no option!"

"No option? Oh, but you're dead wrong on that assumption!" she seethed. "As I've said before, Mr. Malone, *you don't own me!* Now get out of my room so I can change my clothes and get packed—"

"Are you going somewhere?" he drawled lazily.

"You bet I am!" Cassie shouted as she began pulling things from the dresser drawers and flinging them onto the bed.

"I think not!" Steele ground out. His voice was cold and harsh to the girl's ears. His hand folded over hers, preventing her efforts to pack her belongings. He swung her toward him and Cassie froze, staring up into deep, stormy gray eyes that glinted dangerously.

"Let me go!" she hissed, kicking out at Steele with her bare foot, only to meet the resistance of his muscular leg. The blow which hurt her toes had no effect whatsoever on him. "Let me go! My life and what I do with it is no concern of yours!"

"No? Well, think again! You forget, Miss Layton, that it wasn't *I* who asked you into my life! Because I enjoy my life-style, I thought I'd be the last man in the world to spoil it by marriage. I could have left you to the mercy of the world that night you came aboard my yacht! So far as I was concerned, you could have done whatever you pleased so long as you didn't involve me! But you begged me, *begged* me to help you! Do you remember, or shall I refresh your memory?"

Cassie remained silent, humiliated by the mental picture he had conjured up for her. How she had pleaded, had told Steele that she'd do *anything* if he'd help her in what she considered to be a desperate situation.

"My brother walked out, used you, then ran out on you. And I felt sorry for you!" Steele went on. "Well, damn you and your soft brown eyes! Damn you and your body that can stir a man's blood 'til he can no longer concentrate without the thought of it invading his mind!

"Don't think for one moment that I would consider marrying you if I could think of another way out of this mess! But you carry a Malone in that tempting body of yours and the Malone who seeded it there can't claim it or name it. But, by God, this Malone can! And this Malone will! And in doing so, I'll have every damned privilege that goes with it!"

Steele jerked Cassie close to him, staring down at her with eyes dark with smoldering passion. His mouth took hers with a savage, bruising kiss. Cassie refused to open her lips to him and held her body rigid. Steele was trying to hurt her, she thought, trying to punish her.

But even as he damned her and bruised her lips cruelly, Cassie felt the overpowering desire and longing begin to soften her body and mold it to his. Struggling to keep a rein on her wanton self, she freed her mouth from Steele's and threw back her head.

"I hate you!" Cassie's brown eyes blazed the color of amber. "I hate you, hate you, *hate you!*" she cried as tears of frustration spilled down her flushed cheeks.

"Who are you trying to convince, little one, yourself or

me?" Steele's voice was husky with emotion and he still held Cassie clasped tightly in his arms. "I agree that you feel something for me, but I don't believe it is hate!"

"Why—why, you arrogant, pompous jackass—"

Cassie got no further. Steele's lips again claimed hers, his tongue teasing, taking possession of her moist mouth. He crushed her along the length of his masculine hardness, making Cassie all too aware of every hard contour of his rugged body. She wouldn't be able to resist him, she thought, not if he kept on with his slow seduction. She knew this and she was sure that Steele knew it too.

Raising her hands to push free, Cassie's touch met the smooth, tawny flesh that was hot beneath her palms. She felt the crisp mat of hair envelop her fingertips, causing a strange, tingling sensation throughout her yielding body. Cassie felt a raging desire flame deep within her, a desire that seemed to be almost violent, and with sudden clarity she knew that the same urgent need was building within Steele. A fire coursing through their bodies, their veins, a need which cried out to be fulfilled!

It can't happen, she thought frantically, she mustn't let it happen! She wouldn't give in to the weakness of her flesh! She wouldn't have this, not without love, Cassie decided. Oh, yes, she held love for Steele but with love on only one side, it wasn't enough.

With all the strength she could muster, Cassie fought down the waves of sweet torment, the desire that washed over her being, willing herself not to think of the bittersweet pleasure that Steele was drawing from the very seat of her soul.

"No! No, Steele, no! You won't do this to me! You won't!" she choked.

"Then you do admit that you want me!" he demanded thickly. "You want me, Cassie, go ahead and admit it. Admit the passion is there! Admit your need!"

Yes, she wanted him! Dear God, yes! But she would

never admit it, never! If her body would only stop betraying her, she thought fleetingly, if she could just block out the feel of him, the feel of his hands on her heated flesh, forget the taste of his lips—

"Admit that you're on fire, Cassie! That every fiber of your being, every part of your body, is screaming out for fulfillment! Right down to the smallest cell, you're crying out to have me love you!" Steele's arms tightened about her. "Tell me!"

"No! No, it isn't true!" she flung at him in despair. "No!"

"You're lying, Cassie. You're responding to me! God, I can feel you melting in my arms!"

"No, no, no!" Cassie's voice trembled as she choked back her panic.

"You're aching. You're ablaze!"

"Shut up!"

"No, Cassie, not until you admit the truth!" Steele was relentless.

"Steele, please!" she pleaded.

"I'll please you, all right!"

His gray eyes dark with the pain of wanting, Steele pressed her to the bed. Cassie felt the bed push against the back of her knees then, off balance, the two sprawled onto the bed. His weight was heavy upon her, pinning her to the softness of the mattress.

With his fingers entwined in the silkiness of her hair, Steele rolled over and pulled Cassie across his body to settle her atop his hard frame.

"Look at me, Cassie! Look at my body, my mouth, my eyes! Tell me you don't want to touch me! Tell me you don't like the taste of my lips, that you don't want me to want you—to have you!"

He spoke the truth and Cassie knew that this time there was no turning back. She had fought it too often, had dreamed of this moment, and she would be lying if she tried to convince herself otherwise. Steele was the winner. Steele had conquered her!

She lowered her lips to his and a groan of passion and triumph sounded low in Steele's throat. He pulled away from her as he rolled her abruptly to her back and with a ragged oath he hissed through clenched teeth.

"Damn you, Cassie, for making me wait so long!" Covering her body with his own demanding form, Steele kissed her with a tender yet hungry passion and Cassie clung to him, her mouth as demanding as his.

The kiss was suddenly warm, inviting, his tongue searching, yearning for hers until she gave him that for which he was seeking. Steele pressed her deeper into the softness of the bed. They were hungry with desire, each reaching out to the other.

His hands slowly removed the black robe from Cassie's trembling body. Steele's breath came raggedly and with difficulty. His eyes took in the sight of her smooth, silken body and his hands ran the length of her, caressing the warm flesh.

"God, you're beautiful!" The words seemed torn from his lips.

Steele clasped Cassie close to him, his own flesh burning hot against hers. He was a skilled lover, his hands seeking and finding every sensitive point. His fingers brushed the soft inner flesh of her thighs, bringing a quick intake of breath from both of them.

He trailed kisses down her throat to the jutting mounds of her breasts, his tongue tracing the crest of first one, then the other, as his hands fondled and tenderly caressed her. Cassie's breath came in short gasps as she reached out to take his hand in hers.

"Steele, I have to tell you something," she began in a whisper. She was finding it difficult to think clearly because of the sensations his hands were creating. "Steele, about Paul—"

"It doesn't matter, little one. Not now! For the moment, this is all that really matters." His warm fingers traveled ever so slowly up Cassie's smooth thigh to the base of her flat stomach, the tip of one finger sending tiny electric shocks over her quivering flesh.

Again Steele moaned, "This is all that matters!"

Cassie said no more. He would learn soon enough, she thought, but what would happen when he did? What would he say? At the same time these thoughts were running through her mind, another, more urgent, thought struck her. Steele was right! All that mattered was the touch of his hands on her, loving her!

Steele's gray eyes watched her closely in the duskiness, his gaze running freely over her naked body, enjoying each detail, every contour of Cassie's shapely frame.

God, but she was desirable and he was well pleased with what he saw. He knew he'd be equally satisfied with his taste of her for he had hungered for Cassie for far too long, had too long suppressed the urge to partake of her. Now his craving would be appeased.

But at the same time Steele knew that one taste of Cassie wouldn't be enough. One time with her would only temporarily pacify his hunger, for he was certain that the first time would serve only as an appetizer, would stimulate his appetite, and leave him wanting more.

Cassie's lips parted easily, softly, beneath his and Steele muttered a ragged oath as his mouth took hers, his tongue plundering the warm sweetness. Then he raised smoky gray eyes to her face and in that moment, holding her close, he sensed her total surrender, felt her passion, saw her lips parted in open invitation, beheld her naked beauty. Unknowingly, Cassie was seared into Steele Malone's mind and into his heart forever.

"What overpowering passion you have hidden within you, Cassie!" Steele choked huskily, his gray gaze burn-

ing into her, setting her even more aflame. "And to know it can be released at my touch . . ." His words trailed off as his lips ignited a painfully sweet fire within her trembling body.

His hands roamed her flesh and the heat of his touch flowed warmly through her veins. His thumb circled ever so slowly the rosy crest of one yearning breast and the pink-tipped nipple hardened, aching for his mouth to press gently, sweetly, about it.

She was a beautiful creature, an enchanting woman, and Steele longed to answer the unspoken question in her tawny gold eyes. But what was she asking? Other than the need for fulfillment, what did she want from him? What mystery lurked deep within those passion-glazed eyes?

Suddenly he pulled her against him, his lips brushing hers softly, lazily. Then passion built quickly to a peak as his hands worked their magic on Cassie. Featherlike strokes danced along her thighs as his hands caressed the smooth flesh. His weight shifted and his hard body pressed her deeper into the welcome softness of the bed.

Steele's hot lips coursed a trail of burning kisses along her fevered young body, his breath quickening as she responded to his lovemaking. He held her close, but Cassie felt that she wasn't close enough. She clung to him, pressing closer and closer to his heated body, moving against him, luring him.

There was a moment of anguish when Steele rolled away from her, leaving Cassie alone in the middle of the big bed. Was he abandoning her? she wondered in despair. Would he arouse her only to walk away?

Then she heard the soft rustle of his clothing and opened her eyes to see him disrobing. There came the dull thud of his boots as they met the carpeted floor and the smooth, even sound of his zipper.

Cassie studied his male frame gleaming in the darkness, her eyes cloudy dark pools of passion. Then Steele again joined her upon the bed, pulling her to him, his flesh warm against her own. Again his knowing hands soothed her, pleasured her, and Cassie moaned softly in anticipation.

She met Steele with equal desire and a passion so exciting, so full of promise, that it astounded him. The sweet ache within them both was soon to be fulfilled.

His hands firmly on her buttocks, Steele molded Cassie to the length of his body and moved her with him, teaching her the arousing rhythm, guiding her until her own hands began a slow, unsure exploring of his rock-hard body. A delightful shudder claimed her as Steele whispered her name over and over and she felt the throbbing need of his desire hard against her.

Cassie enjoyed the feel of Steele's naked flesh beneath her touch as she stroked his shoulders, his neck, his back. She desired to know him, to know his body, to please him as he pleased her. She reached out to explore, to touch the firm, fevered muscles rippling beneath the flesh. Her hands moved lower, shyly at first, and at his sudden intake of breath she grew braver.

She was startled at the realization that she could make him feel good, could make his body respond to her touch and cause wild excitement to course through him.

Steele's hips were lean, his belly flat and strong. His thighs were smooth and powerful, kindling a new and exciting emotion within her. As Cassie stroked the hard planes of his stomach a shudder ran through him and a groan, almost as if he were in agony, was wrung from deep within his throat.

"My God!" he rasped hoarsely, his voice tight. "Cassie! You're killing me with such sweet torture!"

Steele's lips took hers with such urgency that it took her breath away. His breath was labored and loud as he nibbled at her ear and along her throat, driving her mad with desire. His lips moved on to her breasts to kiss each one, tugging gently at their taut crests, his own sweet form of torture bringing their lovemaking to an intensely torrid height.

Cassie tingled all over and glorious tremors vibrated throughout her body. Her nails dug into his flesh as her need for him grew stronger and her lips sought his. Steele moaned, a husky rattle lodging in his throat, and suddenly he covered Cassie's body completely with his powerful frame, his knee gently urging her to open to him. She yielded willingly, his mouth answering hers with a passionate kiss. He could wait no longer.

Cassie's whimpered cry of pain was lost in the depths of Steele's kiss. Soon the pain eased as he moved gently, deliberately against her and a sudden rush of sweet yearning replaced all else. The primitive need was being fulfilled, the hunger appeased, the thirst quenched.

Cassie's body kept pace with Steele's as she matched the steady, tranquil rhythm of his movements. He held her tightly, his mouth hungry upon hers. His hands lifted to her silken hair, his fingers entangled within the fine silkiness. Her body trembling uncontrollably, Steele's darkened gray eyes met hers and Cassie wished she could read the thoughts smoldering within them.

"You are mine, now, Cassie! Mine!" he whispered with ragged breath and his lips crushed hers.

The passion burst forth as they rode the waves of ecstasy and both were transported by the lofty, sweet emotion. An emotion so intense that neither was capable of rational thought or self-control—and neither cared, as they relished the all-consuming and boundless tide of fulfillment.

10

———eeceeeeeeee———

A virgin!" Steele said in awe.

"I . . . I tried to tell you, Steele, but . . . but you wouldn't listen."

"You started to tell me something about Paul. You said, 'About Paul—'" Steele raised himself to lean on one elbow and stare at Cassie. "But a virgin! Dear God!" He stroked his forehead with the back of his hand.

"You make it sound like some kind of disease," Cassie told him unhappily. "Well, I'm sorry."

"I'm not!" Steele thundered, his gray eyes holding hers. "But, my God, Cassie, you could have warned me, you know!"

"I tried but you didn't want to talk right then." She flushed at the memory.

Steele broke into throaty laughter. "How right you are! But you could have told me."

"So that you wouldn't have made love to me?" Cassie

countered, feeling somewhat hurt. "You wouldn't have, had you known, would you?"

"Oh, I'd still have made love to you, all right! It's just that it would have been different, that's all. Not so much of a shock!" Looking at her intently, Steele asked, "Cassie, are you really so naive that you think that if you had told me then I would just forget what was foremost on my mind? No, I was past stopping, little one! Nothing could have changed my mind. We were both beyond the point of no return." He reached out, stroking the valley between her breasts and a delicious shiver ran through her.

"Then you aren't angry? I mean, you're not upset that I had never—uh—"

"Never gone to bed with a man? No! I'm glad! But it was a shock to find out the way I did. Why didn't you tell me before, when I thought you were not only my brother's lover but Warner's as well?" He gave a low whistle as he suddenly remembered. "And I thought you were pregnant with Paul's child!"

"I had heard you and Helen talking about it that morning and I was angry that anyone could, or would, think such a thing. It upset me but I decided to let you go ahead with your assumption, that no matter what I said, you'd only believe what you chose to believe. And apparently you wanted to believe the very worst of me, that I was the kind of woman that went from one man to another."

When Cassie finished with her explanation, Steele made no reply. He lay back on the bed, his hands beneath his dark head, staring at the ceiling. She wondered what he was thinking, what thoughts were in his mind.

Steele had made love to her with such sweet pleasure, Cassie remembered, helping her to make the transition from a girl to a woman. He had taught her, guided her, and pleasured her. And she had satisfied him, she was sure of it. He had cried out in a ragged voice at his triumph and had shuddered against her, allowing his breathing to return to normal. And he had whispered his fulfillment against her damp hair.

As he remained silent, Cassie could stand it no longer.

"Are you sorry?" she asked in a shy voice.

"Sorry? About what?"

"For making love to me."

"Oh, no! I only wish it had been sooner. Then I wouldn't have gone through all those days of hating Paul for what I thought he had done to you. And hating you because I wanted you. The things I thought about you, Cassie. They weren't very nice."

"I can only imagine!" she replied, then added thoughtfully, "It should make you happy now that you don't have to marry me. Now that you know I'm not pregnant with Paul's child."

"Yes," Steele sighed and Cassie interpreted it to be a sigh of immense relief. "You just don't know how happy!"

Turning, Steele folded her in the warmth of his arms, curving her body to his, and brushed a feather-light kiss on her temple before he whispered, "Why is it that you never went to bed with Paul? It's obvious that he went to bed with the others, that they were, indeed, his mistresses. Why not you?"

Steele was sincere in the query but Cassie was totally unprepared for the question.

"You've asked me more than once if I were naive," she began slowly. "Well, I suppose I am. I'm probably the only twenty-one-year-old virgin around!" The statement brought a hearty laugh from Steele.

"Was!" he corrected. "What just happened between

us makes your being a virgin past tense. And as for you being the only one—well, I'm sure there are others out there your age, or even older."

"Really? Then why was it so hard to believe—so difficult for you to—"

"Because, little one," Steele broke in, "you are the first woman I have ever taken to bed that wasn't already experienced. It isn't my habit to deflower young women!" After a brief pause he asked again, "Why, after the months spent with my brother, didn't—"

"I never had those feelings, those—those emotions—with him, nor with anyone, before," Cassie interrupted him, in a hurry to explain about Paul now that she had the opportunity. Her fingers absently smoothed the fine hair on the back of his hand and she tucked back a stray lock of dark hair which had fallen across Steele's handsome brow before she continued. "And Paul never made any demands on me, there was never any pressure concerning sex. I—again, I was naive, thinking, or rather feeling that he really respected me."

When Steele made no comment, Cassie sighed, releasing a heavy breath, and added, "I thought that he had every intention of marrying me—that he truly loved me!" Her final words were a mere whisper.

Steele lay silent, holding Cassie close in his embrace, his breath warm upon her neck. Could he have understood her reasons for not giving herself to Paul, Cassie wondered. Had he listened, hearing more than she had actually said? She wished Steele knew how very much she loved him, knew how much she wished he would return that love.

She had told him honestly, "I never had those feelings, those emotions." Did Steele know just how much Cassie had given to him, to Steele? It had been much more than her virginity! She had given so much more than that to this man who lay beside her, holding her so naturally within the security of his arms—so much more!

How could she live without him, Cassie asked herself? How could she go for long without having him touch her, love her? What they had had tonight, together, how could he have ever had that with anyone before her?

Then she reminded herself that Steele Malone was a man, a strong, virile man with physical needs and a healthy sexual appetite. And she knew that those needs had been satisfied many times before, knew that he had had an ample supply of women. Steele had been satisfied by women skilled in lovemaking who knew how to please him.

And Cassie had been a girl-woman who had only taken what Steele had given her. She had pleasured in his skills of making love and hadn't known how to give in return.

Her heart cried out to the man who now lay sleeping peacefully at her side. The sound of his deep, even breathing softly reached her ears; his breath fanned the tiny, fine curls on her own brow.

"I love you, Steele Malone, and it scares the hell out of me!" Cassie whispered into her pillow as a single tear coursed its way along her cheek. "I love you and I don't know what to do about it!"

She closed her eyes, bidding sleep, content in Steele's strong embrace.

The cool night breeze wafted through the open window, rippling the soft drapes. The distant sound of the ocean waves as they lapped gently against the shore lured Cassie into drowsiness and, finally, into peaceful slumber.

The two entwined lovers heard nothing as the dim light by the dresser was extinguished. Neither did they see the shadow of a small woman as she crossed the room, her bare feet soundless on the lush carpet. The woman closed the door quietly behind her as she stepped out into the hall, a pleased smile on her kind, aging face.

"Letty, why are my things in Steele's bedroom?"

Cassie's words were flung angrily from the stairway as she reached the bottom step. The housekeeper turned from her dusting, mopping her damp brow with the back of her hand.

"Mr. Steele said I was to put them there, miss," Letty answered matter-of-factly as she resumed her chore of cleaning the rich mahogany coffee table.

So! One night in Steele's arms, one night of sharing the same bed, and the man had moved her into his room to stay! What nerve, what gall he had! Undoubtedly he was the most arrogant, most conceited man she had ever had the misfortune to meet, Cassie stewed.

Well, she wouldn't be installed as his new mistress, she thought furiously. She'd not merely settle into the warmth of his bed and take Helen Thorne's place! One night didn't give him the right to assume that she would do so! That she would gladly and willingly step into the role of Steele Malone's new mistress! Oh, no!

"Well, you can just move them right back where they came from!" Cassie stormed, stamping her small foot on the carpeted step. "God! He is so sure of himself! So confident that after last night—" Her tumbled words came to a sudden halt, her face flushing bright red, as she bit down hard on her lip.

"You mean 'so confident' that after the two of you had become lovers he would take for granted that you'd be movin' into his room with him?"

"We are not lovers!" Cassie shot back, irritated that Letty might have guessed what had happened last night.

"No?" The older woman's graying eyebrow rose questioningly.

"No!" Cassie replied, but the word sounded false, even to her own ears.

"What, then?"

"Well—uh—" Cassie stammered.

"Yes?" the housekeeper prompted.

"We, that is . . ." she floundered to a stop.

"Go on," Letty encouraged.

"Steele . . . I mean, I— Oh, Letty!" Cassie cried out in defeat, sinking to the stairstep and burying her face in her hands.

"It's all right, child." The kindly old woman's voice was gentle and she crossed the room toward Cassie. "There's nothin' to be ashamed of."

"Isn't there?" Lifting her head, Cassie met the pale brown eyes of the little old lady and there she saw tenderness and understanding.

"No, child, there isn't. You love Mr. Steele, don't you?"

"Yes, I love him, but—"

"Then where, pray tell me, is the problem? You wanted him, didn't you?"

"Well, yes, only—"

"Were you ashamed while he held you, while he made love to you?"

"No, of course not, Letty," Cassie answered in a choked whisper.

"They say there's a right time and a right place for everything. Well, I'd say that last night, for you two, was appropriate for that cliché. And, if you don't mind my sayin' so, it should have happened sooner!" With a pert nod of her gray head Letty stressed her statement.

"But, Letty!" Cassie cried out. "Steele shouldn't have made the assumption that I'd just agree to become his mistress! He seems to have taken it for granted that I would simply adapt to that relationship!" Cassie spilled out. "I won't do it! I can't! I'm not cut out for that way of life, that kind of affair!'' Sighing heavily, she pushed back a loose strand of her honey-colored hair. ''I love him, Letty, but I can't—''

The sudden chime of the door bell interrupted and Cassie, still seated at the bottom of the staircase, rose hastily to her feet.

''I'll get it, Letty,'' she told the woman who had resumed her chores but remained near the distraught girl.

Pulling the door wide, Cassie froze and her heart lurched as she stared up into startling blue eyes that held the same shock as her own brown ones.

''Cass!''

''Paul!''

The two names rang out in surprised harmony. Paul Malone dropped his bag on the floor and grasped Cassie in his embrace as he twirled her around, laughing all the while. Then he set her back on her feet and stood looking down at the stunned girl.

''My God, Cass! I've looked everywhere for you! What are you doing here?''

''She lives here!'' Letty spoke up from the background, her voice sharp. ''The question is, what are you doing here?''

''Hello, Letty,'' Paul returned coolly, then proceeded to ignore the woman as he turned back to Cassie. She stood as if rooted to the spot, looking as if she were in a trance. ''Babe, you look swell! Am I glad I found you!'' Again he embraced her, brushing her lips with his own.

Struggling to regain her dignity, Cassie pulled free of Paul and, in a cold, impersonal voice, countered, ''I'd like to hear your answer to Letty's question, Paul. Why are you here?''

''Why, I just came for a visit. An indefinite visit, I might add. My brother does live here, does he not?'' he queried insolently.

''He does.'' It was a flat statement and Cassie turned to

Letty, raising her hand slightly as the housekeeper would have continued.

Paul noted the gesture with a puzzled look, then a cold smile spread across his full lips.

"Mistress of the manor, am I correct?" His tone was nasty and suggestive.

"That she is!" Letty declared proudly. She marched over to Cassie and put her arms about the girl protectively.

Paul chose to pretend that the housekeeper was not even present, his entire attention focused on Cassie.

"It's good to see that you've been well taken care of," he remarked.

"No thanks to *you!*" Cassie spat. "You left me on this island with no money and no friends. You took me for all I had! You lied to me, used me! You despicable—"

"Wait just a minute," Paul broke in smoothly. "You've got it all wrong!"

"Oh, *have* I now! And you are here to tell me differently? Well, you can save your breath, Paul Malone! I don't care to hear anymore of your abominable lies!"

"But I'm not lying, babe, honest! I can explain," Paul wheedled as he stepped toward her. Cassie backed away hastily as he reached out for her.

"Don't touch me!" she screamed. "Don't touch me! Don't speak to me!"

Cassie disengaged Letty's hands as the kindly woman was still holding on to the distressed girl. But as she whirled about to rush up the stairs, she was gripped by Paul's outstretched hand.

"I said I could explain!" he hissed on a low breath. "Just listen to me!"

"Let me go!" Cassie ordered, struggling to pull free of Paul's hold. *"Let go of me!"*

"You heard the lady!" The deep, deadly voice came from the open door behind them.

143

Paul released his grip on Cassie and turned slowly to the source of the voice.

Steele stood in the doorway, cold rage written on his face. Cassie ran to him, flinging her arms about him as she buried her face against his broad chest.

"*Steele!* Oh, Steele!" she cried in sheer relief.

Steele's arms encircled her small trembling body, his hand stroking the silkiness of her hair.

"It's all right, sweetheart," he whispered soothingly against her ear. "It's all right!" Then he spoke to Letty, who stood staring at Paul like an avenging angel. "Letty, please take Cassie to her room and stay with her. I want to talk to my brother."

Without a word the motherly woman came to Cassie and, taking the girl's shaking hand, guided her toward the stairs.

As they passed Paul he reached out and rested his hand on Cassie's shoulder. She stiffened perceptively and her darkened brown eyes flashed first at Paul, then at his hand laying uninvited on her shoulder.

"Cass?" he whispered softly, pleadingly.

"Take Cassie to her room, Letty!" Steele roared.

Cassie sat unsteadily on the side of the bed and Letty knelt to remove the shoes from the trembling girl's feet. So upset was she that Cassie didn't even notice that she had been ushered into Steele's bedroom.

"Why did he have to show up, Letty? Why did Paul have to come back?" the shaken Cassie questioned. "Why must he bring back all the hurt and anger?"

"Don't know, child. I haven't any answers. Young Paul seemed as surprised to see you as you were him."

"I just bet he was!" Cassie rasped angrily. "He hoped never to have to lay eyes on me again, I'm sure. After all, he left me stranded on this—this horrible island with no

144

one to turn to. He didn't know that I would happen to find his brother and that Steele would help me." Her words tumbled out nervously.

"Now, now, miss. You have to get hold of yourself," Letty soothed quietly. "Mr. Steele knows how to handle young Paul. You have nothing to worry about." The woman paused briefly, then continued. "You are a strong young woman, miss, and you'll manage to survive what you feel is a catastrophe. But it really isn't, you know, and you're well able to overcome it. You'll see."

"You—you talk as if I may have to see him again!" Cassie stammered. "I don't want to, Letty! I don't *ever* want to see Paul Malone again!"

"Miss, this is his brother's home, and though there are bad feelings between the two, Mr. Steele would never turn him out. Young Paul said he had come for a visit. He'll tell that to his brother and—"

"And Steele will let him stay! Oh, Letty, I won't be comfortable knowing that Paul could come into my room at any time during the night. He insists on talking to me and I refuse and will continue to do so. But he would see the opportunity after everyone had settled down for the night and he would come to my room! I just *know* he would!"

"Then the safest place for you is right here in Mr. Steele's room. He'll never bother you here," Letty pointed out.

For the first time since she had come back upstairs Cassie was conscious of her surroundings. She was in Steele's bedroom and with the awareness came an odd sense of security. Although she had stormed at Letty for moving her, Cassie's, belongings into this room, had sworn that she would not make the transition, she now viewed the situation in a new light and the room had become a haven for her.

But the fact that Paul, who had so wronged and cheated her, then abandoned her, would be just next door in the only other bedroom suite—

"Oh, Letty! I can't bear it! I can't bear being in this room at night, in Steele's bed, and Paul right in the next room!" she cried hopelessly.

Cassie started at the sudden movement in the doorway. Steele had entered the room as the last desperate words were uttered. The look on his face was evidence that he had heard her final declaration. He stood rigidly, the color draining slowly from his face before being replaced by a deep, angry red.

Without speaking, Steele turned swiftly and left the room.

He had misunderstood her words, Cassie knew he had. And who wouldn't have misunderstood, had they not heard the entire conversation! Oh, Steele, her heart cried out, you didn't understand! He must think I'm still in love with Paul, she thought in wild agitation. He'll think that the shock of seeing him again has reaffirmed my love for his brother! But he was wrong, so very wrong!

"Letty! Steele misunderstood!" Cassie's hands gripped the other woman in distress. "He heard—he only heard—oh, he didn't know what I had been saying before, Letty!"

Cassie broke into a torrent of tears and the kindly old housekeeper pulled her to her breast, cradling her trembling body until the storm of hurt, confusion, and heartache subsided.

11

Cassie leaned back against the massive piece of driftwood that had become her favorite haunt. It was here that she had come following her confrontation with Helen and Steele. It was here that she had first met Troy Warner, here that she came to wrestle with her problems. And it was here that she had found the lovely pink conch shell with Troy's good-bye note.

To Cassie, the aged driftwood had become a friend, and she felt at peace with the familiar touch of the crooked wood which curved about her shoulders. It was as if she had someone to lean on.

Her brown eyes were somewhat glazed as she stared out across the aqua water, and Cassie found it most difficult to get everything into perspective.

Last night she had cried painfully while Letty held her close. She had cried until there were no more tears, yet her heart had gone on weeping, gone on breaking. Even now she felt like crying, but she couldn't. She wanted to scream with frustration, but she wouldn't. Cassie was very unhappy, and very alone.

Looking back, she remembered that when Steele had first attempted to make love to her she had held back and, at his questioning, had declared that Paul was her reason for doing so. She had planted the seed of doubt deliberately, causing Steele to believe that she still loved Paul, and she had never told him differently. So it had been only natural that Steele had misconstrued her words last night, Cassie sighed regretfully.

It had been very late, way past midnight, when Steele had finally come upstairs. He hadn't spoken to Cassie, hadn't known that she was wide awake and that she wanted to talk to him, to explain.

Steele had entered, going straight to the bathroom where he had showered for a seemingly interminable time. Returning to the bedroom, he had settled himself in the chair by the window where he sat in silence, smoking incessantly, for what had seemed hours. Cassie, faking sleep, lay quietly, not daring to move. She had shed silent tears, bathing her cheeks and pillow.

Eventually Steele had stood and walked over to the bed, where he paused for a moment staring down at her; then with a heavy sigh he had quietly left the room. He didn't return that night and Cassie had lain there in the darkness waiting for him, listening intently for his footsteps. But he had not come back. And when sleep finally came, her last remembered heartbreaking thoughts were that she would not have the warmth of Steele's body next to her, that there would be no gentle words, no tender caresses.

Now Cassie watched the whitecapped waves as they rolled into shore only to scurry back out again. She thought how they seemed to parallel her emotions. The waves seemed uncertain as to where they wanted to remain. Her aching heart was unsure of her own desired love.

The luring motion of the waters seemed to beckon the sun, beseeching the golden orb to slip into their waiting, blue-green depths. A soft breeze blew gently, lightly stirring the soft, sun-bleached sand.

Cassie closed her eyes to blot out all but the sensation of the cool wind upon her skin, the sweet-scented aroma of the island, and the peaceful, swishing echo of the ocean waves.

"Cass?" The voice was a mere whisper upon the wind.

Cassie started, her once-relaxed body stiffening at the recognition of the smooth voice. She made to rise but Paul's hand rested on her arm as he knelt down beside her.

"Please, Cass! Don't go! I have to talk to you," he implored in a choked whisper. "I—I have to explain!"

"Explain? There is nothing to explain, Paul! Nothing you have to say could possibly make any difference to me!" Cassie flung tartly, jerking her arm from him.

"You're wrong, babe. I can—"

"No, *you're* wrong, Paul. I do *not* want to talk to you! Can't you understand?" she bit out sharply, her brown eyes fiery. "I want nothing more to do with you! Not *now*—not *ever!*"

"But it wasn't my fault, Cass, honest!"

"Not your fault? My God!" Cassie jumped to her feet, her brown gaze burning down at him. "Not your fault! Hah!" She gave a short, bitter laugh.

"I came back to the hotel," Paul began hurriedly. "But you were gone—had checked out. I looked for you, babe, but I couldn't find you. I asked the desk clerk and he said you had checked out!"

"You are the one who had checked out," she countered, her voice shaking. *"You deserted me!"*

"I left the hotel, yes, but only to go to the boat," Paul explained, rising to his feet. His hands reached out, grasping Cassie's, as he went on. "But, no, Cass, I didn't desert you. I came back for you!"

"I'm the one who went to the boat, Paul, not *you! You* lied! *Malone's Passion* isn't your boat, it's your brother's. And you never went there, Steele was the only Malone there! That's just another of your lies!"

"Okay, so I lied about owning the boat. But I had to, Cass, please believe me!" he pleaded as Cassie pulled her hands free and turned abruptly to walk away from him.

"Believe you?" she flung over her shoulder, hastening her steps. "Believe you when all you've ever done is lie to me, deceive me? No, thank you, Paul Malone, save your pleas for someone else!"

"It was Steele!" Paul yelled desperately, causing Cassie to stop in her tracks. She didn't turn to look at him and Paul took a few, uncertain steps toward her. Sensing that he had her full attention, Paul pushed his advantage. "It was Steele," he repeated. "He was the one who forced me to leave you, to lie to you! It was Steele who—"

"No!" Cassie choked, refusing to believe it.

"It was, I swear it! He's a dangerous man, babe, a strong man. He's had a private investigator following me for months. Steele knew I was here—with you. And he came after me." Paul ran his fingers along his temples and took a deep breath before he continued. "Cass, I'm married. I have been married for over four years. Lynn won't give me a divorce and that's why I had to stall all this time about you and me getting married. I was playing for time, hoping she would eventually give in. But she won't, and Steele is on her side. Lynn sent him after me!"

Cassie turned slowly toward Paul, noting the stricken

look on his boyish face, his pleading blue eyes. Incredible though it sounded, could it be that he spoke the truth. She wanted to believe that Paul had loved her, that he had not willfully deserted her. But she realized that it was her pride overruling her good sense; no woman wanted to suffer the humiliation of having a man walk out on her, toss her aside, no longer wanting her.

"I don't believe you!" Cassie stated flatly.

"But, Cass, it's the truth!"

"Oh, I know there's truth to your being married, that a private investigator has been following you, and that Steele is responsible for his doing so," Cassie began, choosing her words carefully. "I also believe that your wife won't give you a divorce. And I believe that Steele is dangerous, that he is a strong man. But there, Paul, is where the truth ends!"

Paul opened his mouth to speak but Cassie stopped him with an upraised hand and a violent shake of her head. "No! Let me finish. It's your time to listen! I don't believe that Steele forced you to desert me, to just walk off and never look back. And I don't believe that he forced you to lie to me!" she concluded.

"What you mean is that you don't want to believe Steele to be capable of all this. You're refusing to see him as he really is!" was Paul's angry rejoinder.

"I know the kind of man he is!" Cassie snapped heatedly. "And for all that he is, Steele Malone is no liar! He is what he is—strong, powerful and, yes, dangerous —because he is truthful!"

"So you're on his side, too!" Paul snarled. "Steele has always been everybody's favorite! He's always had everything, even when we were kids! It was he who was loved best and always got his way about everything! He never wanted me to have *anything*—not mother's love, nor dad's approval! When things went wrong or something was broken, Steele pointed the finger at me and

151

they always took his word. I got the blame! He's always wanted whatever I had! He never wanted me to have something *he* didn't have. Steele saw you, Cass. He saw you and he wanted you. Ol' Paul's found him a beauty he thought, a woman who's worth something, and Steele had to have you because it was something I had and he didn't! You were mine and he couldn't stand it! He had to have you! Now, can't you see all that?''

All of Paul's spite and jealousy had been spilled out in just a few brief moments. His own inferiority and years of feeling dominated by his older brother had embittered him and caused him to be resentful of Steele's accomplishments, Cassie knew, yet she found herself wondering if there might be a thread of truth in what Paul had said.

Dear God! Was it possibly true? Could it be that Steele only wanted her because he thought she belonged to Paul? She didn't want to believe it, yet the insistence in Paul's voice seemed to reach out to her. But at the same time she didn't want to believe what Paul was saying about Steele. She knew Steele, did she not? She had seen his honesty, had witnessed his gentleness. She had felt the tenderness and the warmth that flowed deep within him.

Cassie couldn't believe, *wouldn't* believe, that she had fallen in love with Steele only to learn that he was not the man she wanted him to be, had trusted him to be.

Yet she had stood mutely, with mixed emotions, as she had listened to Paul. She had seen the hurt in his handsome face when he talked about his brother. But her heart, as well as her mind, kept warning her, calling out to her to believe in Steele.

Think, Cassie! Think! she admonished herself. Why would Steele Malone want his brother's woman? Why, when Steele had all the women he wanted and a lot more than he needed! Something was terribly wrong, she decided, there must be more to all this than she had just heard. It was not necessary for a man like Steele to have to go to such extremes to get what he wanted, not when it was a woman!

Cassie was lost in her own thoughts and did not hear Paul's rambling words, his further incrimination of Steele, and his acid remarks about his brother. Only when she heard her name spoken in desperation did she bring her thoughts back to the persistent Paul.

"Please, Cass! Please, babe, don't let him get away with it! Not this time! Listen to me, trust me! Steele's gone to a lot of trouble to make you believe that I deserted you. He even told me to tell you the story about the boat. It was all Steele's idea. Then he called me at the hotel and told me to return to Miami, go back to Lynn that night. If I refused, he told me I'd be left without a cent! He said he'd take away all that I had coming from dad's inheritance. And he could do it, Cass, he is the executor of the estate!

"He was blackmailing me, babe! He threatened to go to court with Lynn and testify against me! Against his own flesh and blood! I'd be stripped, left with nothing! He also threatened to bring out what the investigator had learned. He said he would drag us to court, Cass, you and me. He would make our love, our relationship, something dirty and help Lynn take our child away from me. Steele would go so far as to take my job away from me, throw me out of the company. The business our family has had for years!"

Although she didn't want to hear all that Paul was saying, it seemed to Cassie that the words were indelibly imprinted upon the screen of her mind and she knew that in the days to come she would go over them again and again.

Now desperate, Paul's voice had become high-pitched. "I left you a note that night, Cass. I gave it to the desk clerk but Steele intercepted it. In my note I explained everything, told you why I had to leave so unexpectedly. Even left some money in the envelope for you to get back to Miami and an address where you could reach me. But Steele told the clerk to tell you only that I had gone, checked out. Damn it, Cass, Steele owns that hotel and the hired help take his orders without question. God! He covered every angle, every out!"

So mystified was Cassie, so dumbfounded by the revelations that Paul was making with such sincerity, that her mind was whirling with all the accusations.

Paul had neatly stacked the evidence against Steele but wasn't a man considered innocent until proven guilty beyond the shadow of a doubt? And doubt was certainly battling against the statements Paul had made.

Her mind in tumultuous confusion, Cassie knew that she couldn't take any more of this. She had to get away from Paul, away from his resounding voice, away from his pleas. Her head was spinning and a pain was stabbing somewhere in the region of her heart.

"No more!" she screamed. "No more, Paul!" Cassie covered her ears tightly with her hands. "Oh, God! Please don't let it be true! *Please, Steele, don't have lied to me!*" Her own desperate pleas were sent heavenward as scalding tears drenched her flushed cheeks.

"Steele? Don't let *Steele* have lied to you?" Paul shot at her, his eyes coldly, darkly blue. "Is Steele all you're worried about? What about us, Cass? What about you and me?"

"There is no 'us'! There is no 'you and me'!" Cassie cried out in scornful contempt.

With that, she fled the unpleasant scene, her bare feet leaving only shallow prints in the sand.

Paul was left in the wake of Cassie's hasty departure, a lonely figure on the deserted, darkened beach.

Cassie sat staring out the bedroom window. She had not seen Paul after her abrupt departure from the beach. Steele had not returned and Cassie had found the house empty and lonely and had paced the floor restlessly until Letty had come in with her groceries.

"Let this wait, Letty," Cassie had said breathlessly, taking the bags from the other woman's arms and depositing the groceries on the wide counter. "I have to talk to you."

And she had. Cassie had told Letty everything. The whole conversation, word for word, as she remembered it. She had seen the stunned surprise on the older woman's face and couldn't help but recall her own defense of Steele.

"I know the kind of man he is!" she had flung in Paul's face. "And for all that he is, Steele Malone is no liar!" Her own words were repeated over and over in her mind. Yet there was so much that Paul had said that could be true, couldn't it?

"I don't believe one word of it!" Letty snorted. "And I thought you knew Mr. Steele well enough not to believe it either!"

"But, Letty—" Cassie began.

"Don't 'but, Letty' me, child! After all young Paul has done to you, you're going to stand there and read truth into his poisonous words. I love the boy, but I know him. I helped raise him! He has never known what it was to tell the truth." Letty paused and reached to take Cassie's hands in her own. "I can say all the right words, give you every reason not to believe young Paul and to believe in Mr. Steele," she explained quietly. "But it's not Letty you have to trust, miss. No, you have to make up your own mind. What does your heart say? What does your own good judgment say?"

"I don't know! I just don't know!" Cassie sighed wearily, shaking her honey-colored head. "The only way I'll know for sure is to confront Steele and ask him for his side of the story!"

"If that's what you feel is right, then that's what you'll have to do, miss, only—" Letty broke off.

"Only what?"

"Well, just don't be surprised at how Mr. Steele will react. That boy's a proud one and he might take it wrong. You may lose all the way around!"

Cassie had never doubted that she had met Steele Malone by accident, that he had helped her because he hadn't agreed with the shabby way his brother had treated her. But now that Paul had come back—oh, she didn't know what to believe any more, didn't know whom she could trust!

Dragging herself to her feet, Cassie crossed to the bedroom door, but as she reached for the knob the door opened and Steele filled the doorway with his large, powerful frame. His white silk shirt was carelessly unbuttoned, his tie and jacket hung over his arm.

He looked tired, Cassie thought. Even his eyes that seemed always alive with gray mystery were dull and his dark hair was unruly.

"Hello, little one," Steele greeted her and a tender smile touched his lips as he bent easily and placed a gentle kiss on Cassie's forehead. "It really is nice to come home to someone like you!" he remarked, walking over to the bed where he sank wearily upon it and began to unbutton the cuffs of his shirt.

Cassie, taken aback by his tenderness, remained in the open doorway, a look of uncertainty on her lovely face.

This wasn't a man who took advantage of another for his own gain, she realized. There was so much more to Steele Malone than she would ever know, ever understand.

He had never led her to believe anything other than that which was there, in plain view for her to see. He had been so open about everything. But still, Cassie felt that she had to remove the seeds of doubt which Paul had planted before they took firm root and began to grow. She had to set her mind at ease by knowing the real truth, then she would go on from there. And if Letty were right and she did lose him, then it was just a chance she had to take.

"Steele?" Cassie whispered unevenly.

"Hmmm?" was his answer as he lay back on the bed, stretching his lithe body. His muscles rippled as he flexed his shoulders to ease the tautness.

Turning his head toward her, Steele smiled his familiar crooked smile, the silver-gray lights again dancing in his eyes.

With a deep intake of breath, Cassie began. "I was on the beach this afternoon. I went there to think, as I do a lot of times. Paul followed me and—"

Steele sat upright, his body rigid, his anger obvious.

"Did he persuade you to come back to him? Did he proclaim his undying love?" His voice was bitter, his tone icy cold. "Did he admit that he had hurt you, then kiss you, and make it better?"

"Steele, why do you hate Paul so much?" Cassie had had no intention of asking the question, it had tumbled out before she had time to stop it.

"You can ask such a question? After all that you know about him, after what he has done?" Steele demanded. Then in a low, weary voice he told her, "I don't hate my brother, Cassie. It's just that we are two very different

157

types. We don't live by the same standards, the same rules. The more distance we keep between us, the better off we both are."

Steele ran tanned fingers through his thick black hair, then dropped both hands to his knees and sat staring at the floor.

"He came back for you," he told Cassie softly, without looking up. "You are the reason Paul's here."

"But he didn't even know I was here! He was surprised to see me!"

"No, he wasn't surprised to see you. He knew you were here."

"How? How did he know?" Cassie asked curiously, crossing the room to stand before Steele.

"I told him," he answered matter-of-factly. "It was a mistake on my part. However, as it turned out, it didn't really matter. He already knew where you were before I told him, Cassie." Steele raised painful gray eyes to look into her wide brown eyes. "Helen called Paul as soon as she hit Miami," he sighed. "She wanted to blast my whole plan, wanted it to blow up in my face!"

"Plan? What plan, Steele?" Cassie whispered chokingly, her heart beating wildly in her breast. Was he admitting to what Paul had accused him, she wondered frantically. Had it, after all, been true?

"I had a plan but it doesn't matter now," he replied, his gaze still holding hers. "I thought I knew best and I took things into my own hands. Now I know how wrong I was to do so. But at the time, I felt I was right, little one."

Cassie's legs had begun to tremble and her knees felt as if they had turned to jelly. She sank slowly to the floor and sat staring at Steele as she began her interrogation.

"Steele, did you know about Paul and me before we came to Nassau?"

There was a brief silence before Steele answered.

"Yes," he said simply.

"Did you have a private investigator following us? Spying on us?"

"Yes."

"Have you threatened Paul with the loss of his job, his child, his—"

"I have!"

"Did you tell him that you would go to court with the information which this investigator had gathered?"

"I did."

Cassie was thankful that she was sitting on the floor because she knew that her legs would never have supported her had she remained standing. It was true, all of what Paul had said was true! She was staggered that not only had Steele admitted it, but he had not hesitated to answer her questions, not for the tenth of a second.

The room was gripped by an unnatural silence. It seemed to Cassie that she was viewing the scene from a far distance. Her mind was in a turmoil and her heart was aching unbearably.

With a valiant effort she regained her composure and began her narrative, relating her conversation with Paul. All the while, Cassie was watching Steele closely but he only sat listening intently, making no attempt to interrupt, no effort to clarify or to justify.

The story Paul had told her was still very vivid in her mind and Cassie had no difficulty in repeating everything. She left out not one iota of the memorable conversation.

When she had finished, Cassie studied the silent Steele as his darkened gray eyes traveled over her worried face, his own face unreadable. Then he rose to his feet and stooped to lift Cassie to hers.

Gathering her into his strong arms, Steele's lips sought Cassie's, taking them in a gentle, yet deliberate, kiss that sent her blood racing and brought her body closer, molding it to Steele's hard length. He released her and stood for a moment stroking her cheek with his hand, his fingers tracing the softness of her lips. Then he set her from him and walked out the door.

Cassie sagged to the bed, shaken by her emotions, her senses reeling from Steele's kiss. Suddenly it didn't seem to matter what Steele might have done. It didn't matter to what lengths he might have gone to come between her and Paul because she realized that she had never loved Paul. And she did love Steele, loved him with an unfathomable depth.

All of the faults she had found in Steele miraculously faded away and Cassie could look beyond them to the man himself. She had wanted him from the first, and now that she was in his life, no matter how small a part she might play or why she was there at all, Cassie didn't want to let go.

She looked up as Steele came back into the room. In his hand he held a thick manila folder and he strode toward her with animal grace. A tremor ran through Cassie as she regarded him. He was beautiful, she thought, her heart wanting him to realize her great love for him. Had she lost him? The thought struck terror to her young heart and she felt chilled. Could it possibly be that she had lost him just as she had really found him?

Steele tossed the folder on the bed next to her and when she looked up at him in question, he smiled and said simply:

"Before you read that, before you draw any conclusions or make any decisions, would you please answer one question for me, Cassie Layton? Will you do that much?"

Cassie nodded mutely and Steele resumed.

"That night when I first wanted to make love to

you—was it really your love for Paul that held you back?"

"No," she whispered honestly, her eyes pleading for his understanding.

"Then *why?* Why did you stop me?"

"Because—" Cassie began in a strangled voice. "Because I—I was afraid! Afraid of what I was feeling . . ." She trailed off into silence.

Steele waited quietly, asking no further questions, knowing that Cassie had to think it through for her own sake. Then she spoke, her words whispered.

"I—I had this fear, this feeling that if—if I ever gave in that I'd—I'd never want to break free." A solitary tear found its way down her cheek.

Steele dropped to one knee before Cassie and, gently cupping her chin in his hand, he looked at her with inscrutable gray eyes. That same electric spark was there between them, the mysterious tide that seemed to flow from one to the other, the breathless anticipation.

For a moment Cassie thought that Steele was going to take her in his arms but he didn't. Looking deep into her eyes, he spoke with truth and sincerity, his words full of meaning.

"I only ask that you give freely what you have to give. I ask nothing more, nothing less. I want those feelings, whatever they may be, to be given wholly and without hesitation, without reservation. I will never ask more of you. I could have made you promises, Cassie. Promises which I could not keep.

"But I didn't believe that you wanted that. So I made no promises then and I'll make no promises now. I wanted you very much, Cassie, and I still do, but you have to realize that I'm not the monster that Paul has made me out to be, the ogre you seem to believe that I am."

Steele's smoky gray eyes moved to the folder which Cassie now held in her hand. He stood and pointed a finger at the thick file.

"Read that," Steele said abruptly. "Read it and then make your decision. It is up to you to decide who is right and who is wrong."

With those parting words, Steele turned and walked rapidly from the room, leaving Cassie staring down at the blank front of the large manila folder.

Suddenly it seemed alive in her hands and she was actually afraid to open it. What would she find inside, she wondered uneasily, what secrets were hidden there to be unveiled before her eyes? Who would be hurt by information which lay beneath the tan paper shelter?

With shaking fingers Cassie leafed back the cover and with a sense of foreboding, she began to read.

12

~~~~~~~~~~~~~~~~

Cassie finished reading the last report and closed the file, her fingers holding it in a deathlike grip. What she had found inside it was all the proof she had needed. The file contained a full year of investigative information and had been compiled by more than one private investigator. There were dates, locations, occasions and women's names, five, to be exact, and one of the names was her own. Each woman's past and present had been professionally examined and a report made thereon.

The first, a lovely blonde named "Della," had lived in New York. Paul had met her at a party and the two had slipped away unobserved to seek the privacy of Della's plush apartment. They had become lovers that same night, the report stated. The relationship terminated three months later and Paul left a distraught Della pleading with him to come back to her. The final scene took place in a public night club. From this liaison Paul had obtained two exquisite diamond rings, a gold watch, and several thousand dollars.

Then, one week later, came Terri James. She had stepped into an elevator at Malone Enterprises where Paul had been the sole occupant. As the car descended there was a power failure and the two had been trapped between floors for half an hour. At the end of which time they had become very well acquainted and the ensuing affair lasted two months to the day. Paul's tactics had been identical to those used with Cassie, conning the pretty redhead into selling all her belongings. They flew off to Bermuda where, of course, Paul had left her.

It was on the plane from Bermuda to Miami that Misty Howard took the seat next to the handsome young playboy. They became quite chatty on the flight and upon their arrival to Miami, Misty accepted Paul's suggestion that she share his taxi. After dinner and a few drinks, the pert young brunette invited him to her beachfront apartment for a nightcap. The two did not emerge from this hideaway for two days. Then Paul moved in and stayed just four days short of three months. This relationship supplied him with a new car, flashy clothes, and an undetermined amount of cash.

During this romantic interlude Paul had played a dual role. A singer in a popular Miami night spot, Misty worked nights and romped with Paul during the day. And at night Paul was keeping Misty's younger sister occupied. The blonde beauty, a widow of only six months, was very lonely and out of touch with people of her own age, having married a man thirty years her senior. All that Widow Carla had left in this cruel world was a well-padded bank account from good old John's inheritance. And Paul had made good use of it for four months, the longest of his recorded affairs.

Probably, Cassie thought with disgust, Carla had had the most to offer, not only her body and her beauty, but

Paul's number one interest—money! This breakup was brought about when "big brother" Steele crashed their engagement party and calmly announced that Paul's wife had been taken to the hospital to have their baby, was in the labor room at that moment, and that Paul's immediate presence was expected.

"Exit Carla, stage left. Enter Cassandra Layton, stage right," Cassie intoned dramatically.

It was all there, every last detail. From the beginning of each sordid affair to the end. The days, the nights, the weeks and months of the life and times of Paul Malone!

What made Cassie most furious was to realize that she had fallen for his smooth con act, not once, but *twice!* From his pleading blue eyes, his stricken, forlorn face and his trembling hands right down to his wavering, breaking voice, Paul Malone was a first-class actor!

And Cassie had been taken in again, this time to the degree that it had caused her to have grave doubts about the man she loved. She had doubted his honesty, his intentions, his integrity.

"Have you learned enough?" The soft question drifted across the dimly lit room and Cassie looked up to see Steele closing the door quietly behind him. "If not, there's more." He lifted his hand which held two more thick binders. "These were in the library safe and they contain an additional two years of the accounts of my dear brother's activities." With a smile Steele added, "And mine!"

Cassie smiled to herself at the last two words. "And mine," Steele had pointed out. Yes, he had been there in the reports. Steele Malone had woven in and out, stepping in at exactly the right time. But, according to what she had read, Cassie Layton had been the only woman in Paul's wild life with whom Steele had ever become personally involved.

Oh, he had made the arrangements for Terri James's

flight back home from Bermuda and had given her sufficient funds to restore her life to order. He had seen to it that Misty Howard's car had been returned to her, along with what money Paul had left. But he had taken Cassie Layton under his wing!

"I've read enough!" she whispered, her gaze resting on the folders in Steele's strong hand. "In fact, I believe I've read more than enough!"

"And?" he asked softly, stepping closer.

"And—and I—oh, Steele! I'm so sorry!" Cassie choked, her heart breaking. She desperately wanted to reach out, to touch this man whom she loved so dearly, so achingly. But she restrained herself. "I should never have doubted you, not when you've always been so straightforward with me! Right from the start—that first night on the boat. Forgive me, understand—"

"I understand, little one," he said gently. His hand was warm as he touched her cheek tenderly. "I understand more than you know."

"Steele?" The one word was spoken with deep passion and Cassie stared up into his gray eyes, eyes which held volumes of emotion and mystery.

"Yes, Cassie?"

"There was—well, on each report there was a photo of the woman on whom the report was made," she began uncertainly, moistening her dry lips with the tip of her tongue. "And on the report—the one on me, there wasn't a picture. Why?" Cassie wanted to know.

Steele smiled his disarming, crooked smile that always made Cassie seem to melt on the inside, her pulse change its tempo and her heart beat frantically out of control.

"Does it really matter whether or not there was one?" His smile held amusement.

"W—well," Cassie faltered, "I don't know that it exactly matters, it's just that I was curious."

"All right, there was one—rather, there is one," Steele informed her. He laid the folders on the dresser before he turned and gazed at Cassie for a long moment. "Do you know just how beautiful you are? Are you even aware of what your beauty can do to a man?"

Cassie wasn't sure how to answer, and the pure richness of his vibrant voice, together with his complimentary words, sent a pleasant sensation along her veins. She stared at Steele silently, deciding that he didn't expect an answer.

"In all honesty, I can say that I have never in my life wanted anyone the way I do you," Steele continued. "I wanted you, Cassie, long before I even met you. You, your face haunted me, even followed me into my dreams. I knew I'd have no peace until I had you."

His hand made a slow descent to the back pocket of his black trousers and, retrieving his leather wallet, Steele opened it and flipped through the plastic inserts. Then he stood staring down at it as he went on talking.

"This was handed to me the day Hall brought his first report on Paul. His latest 'mistress,' Cassandra Layton, is the way he introduced me to this lovely image." He paused and glanced briefly at Cassie. "After he left, I must have sat for hours, staring at your beauty—your sherry brown eyes stared back, the pouty mouth taunted me, enticed me. I ran a finger along that jawline so often that I imagined that I could actually feel silken skin, could feel the warmth from the flesh."

Steele drew a deep, ragged breath as he handed the billfold to Cassie. Her brown eyes beheld those same brown eyes looking back at her. She couldn't believe that Steele had been carrying her picture with him all this time. Steele tucked the wallet back into the pocket of his trousers.

"But why?" she managed, more confused now than ever.

167

"You really don't know, do you, little one? You truly don't understand. You have absolutely no idea what torment I'd gone through all those weeks before you literally tumbled onto the deck of my boat that night." Steele chuckled at the memory, then went on more seriously. "I went through pure hell the times I held you in my arms. You were so close, yet so far from me."

With an agonized groan Steele reached down and took Cassie's face to cup her chin in his big hand as his smoky gray eyes peered deep into hers, so deep that she believed he could almost see her very soul.

"I—I—" Cassie stammered, swallowing with difficulty, "Steele, I—"

"I wanted only what you were willing to give, my haunting beauty," he broke in. "But, just as you have admitted that you are afraid, I, too, am afraid. Afraid that once you had given yourself to me, once I'd had you, that *I* would never again be free. You're right about me, you know, I am arrogant, overbearing and possessive. But those things—like having my way and always finishing something once I've started it—it's my nature! Oh, God, Cassie!"

Steele took her mouth with urgency, his fingers entwined in the honey silk of her hair. His mouth moved with deliberate, tranquil seduction and his body trembled, pressing toward Cassie with a growing need.

And Cassie responded, her arms encircling Steele's neck, her own mouth hungry for him. His deep, throaty moan sent tiny electric shocks coursing along her body. She sensed the power she had over him, the passion she was able to stir within him. But at the same time, she knew that Steele held that same power over her, stirring a passion that equaled his own.

"Steele, please!" Cassie whispered against his burning lips.

"Do you remember what happened the last time you

said that?" he asked in a husky voice, his breath teasing her senses. "I told you, 'I'll please you, all right.'" His breathing was short and ragged, his body taut as a spring wound too tightly.

"I—I can't think when you're doing this," she protested weakly.

"Then don't think!"

"But there are things I need to know, things I want to understand."

"All you need to know is that I want you," Steele murmured against her shoulder. His hands were now traveling over her body, his swift, sure fingers working the buttons of her blouse. Reaching inside, he claimed the firm, waiting mounds that ached for his touch. And when he spread his hands over her tender breasts, cupping and caressing them, Cassie thought she would go mad with the intensity of her desire.

What was it she had wanted to ask Steele? What were those things she needed to know and understand? They no longer mattered, she no longer cared, and Cassie felt herself surrendering, molding to the solid form of Steele.

The forgotten report files fell from her lap to the floor, the papers scattering in careless disarray. Cassie abandoned all thoughts but Steele and his wanting her, and lay back on the bed.

"Yes, my beauty, yes," came Steele's passion-filled voice as he followed, his long body stretching out beside her. "Want me! Need me!" he urged.

Cassie's eager hands fumbled with the buttons on his shirt as her wanton body arched toward him. Steele tugged at the shirt, pulling the tails free of his pants. Then he grasped both Cassie's searching hands in one hand and looked down into eyes the color of smoky topaz.

As their eyes met and held, her breathing came in sharp, panting gasps. And Steele gloried in her surrender, the expression on his face told Cassie this. He smiled, the dimple in his cheek showing noticeably, his teeth tugging at his lower lip as he slowly unbuttoned his shirt. A dark lock of hair fell forward to dangle upon his forehead.

Cassie did want him, did need him. And that's all that mattered now, this moment of getting closer to Steele. So close that she could feel the pounding of his heart. She wanted only to respond to his caress, to have this desire fulfilled. This raw desire that was fast building within her, this savage hunger must be satisfied, the fierce thirst quenched once more.

This primitive behavior that Steele could so easily, so effortlessly, bring to the surface was sweet torment, and Cassie felt that she would die from the bittersweet pain if he didn't soothe her, stroke her, satisfy her soon.

"Please, Steele, please!" This time the words were not a plea for him to stop but whimpered words of persuasion.

Steele pulled Cassie to him, his body enveloping hers. She could feel the lean, taut muscles, the crisp mat of hair on his chest beneath her fingers. Her body trembled at his touch as he stroked her silken flesh and kneaded her frame to his.

His teeth nibbled gently at her throat, his strong fingers danced lightly over her whole body. He entwined his legs about her, crushing her closer to him, and moved the palm of his hand over her breast, cupping it, teasing the rosy crest until the sensitive nipple responded, hardened, and swelled with passion beneath his touch. Steele knew all too well how to arouse her, how to please her.

He planted kisses along Cassie's cheek, neck, and shoulder. The desire, the familiar urgency was building within them both, coursing through their veins like wildfire. Steele's eager mouth covered hers, his tongue parting her soft lips, and he drank the warm sweetness of her kiss.

His lazy strokes awakened every nerve in her body and a purely animal moan came from within her as his kiss became more demanding. Her lips were tender and yielding, her heart and body cried out to be taken. There was a bittersweet yearning in her young body, a passion which she knew that only he could satisfy.

Now his lips were tracing her fevered body, his mouth gentle and soft as he placed moist warm kisses along her breasts, her narrow waist, her belly and thighs. His tongue was as practiced, as experienced, as were his hands.

Suddenly Cassie wanted to return the sensation, wanted to touch him as he was touching her. She wanted Steele to experience the same sweet emotions. She pushed gently at his shoulders, urging his body away from her. His movements stilled and he looked down at her, his passion-darkened eyes questioning.

Steele became rigid, his breath ragged and heavy. God, but he wanted her, was eager for her! He needed her and the need was so strong, so overwhelming, that it left him soulless from wanting Cassie.

"Steele?" she whispered huskily, her hands pressed against his broad chest. "Steele, I—" The words died away and Cassie bit down on her lower lip.

Steele attempted to control his breathing, to relax, to still the rising emotions. Slowly, reluctantly, he rolled from her and onto his back. But to his utter surprise Cassie followed. Her mouth quickly upon his, she kissed him deeply, wantonly, and he clasped her to him.

"Cassie, Cassie." The name was a muffled cry.

Cassie felt Steele's body respond, heard his breathing deepen, the ragged calling of her name and knew that she had done right. She was now the one giving pleasure. It was her fingers, moving lightly over his shoulders and along his rib cage, that evoked the husky moans from Steele. Her fingertips were spreading a

171

raging fire within him, bringing forth excitement and the sweet pain of passion.

His body was no longer still, the rigidness of his frame was taut with his need and his effort to remain in control of his passion was failing completely.

Cassie's hands moved over him slowly, effortlessly. Her tongue teased the corners of his mouth, her small teeth nibbled at his under lip. Then her mouth followed the trail her hands had made over Steele's rock-hard frame.

A fine film of sweat covered his body, glistening in the darkness. The tangy taste of salt was upon her lips and tongue and the taste was warm and sweet. The musky, sensual smell of Steele invaded her nostrils, pleasing her senses.

Steele buried his fingers in Cassie's hair, urging her lower. His breath came faster, more labored, and his body arched with her tranquil movements. She was arousing him to the very core of his being.

Cassie's tongue made a slow, circular motion along the hollow of his belly, moving on to outline the fine hairline running the length of his flat stomach. The action brought a sudden, sharp intake of breath from Steele and again he whispered her name.

His abdomen quivered at the warm, moist touch of her tongue and his hands began to move to Cassie's shoulders. His tanned fingers massaged gently, yet with strength, as they moved over her back and neck. He was a master with his hands, Cassie had thought many times, but the arousing movements of those hands were somehow different as he rubbed and stroked her this time. They were in rhythm with her own hands upon his body and, even as she pleased him, he was pleasing her.

So this was the way, this was what loving was all about! It wasn't a one-way street! It was a mutual thing—both giving, both receiving! It was wonderful and beautiful and far beyond her wildest imaginings. She was learning. Steele had taught her well.

His grip tightened about her slender shoulders and with little effort he pulled Cassie's body over the length of him, settling her astride his large frame. Looking down into his dark eyes, Cassie saw more than mere passion, more than lust or desire. But what was it? She urged her mind to answer. Then Steele smiled disarmingly and, if possible, her heart beat faster.

"This is what matters between lovers, Cassie. This emotion, these feelings. Have you now experienced them, little one? Do you know now what they are?" Steele spoke with difficulty. "Do you?"

"Yes, Steele," Cassie answered honestly. "Yes, I now know!"

"Then love me, love me as I have you."

And Steele's lips sought hers, crushing her to him, moved her with him, teaching her yet another new experience, a new way to make love.

Later, their bodies in the gentle stilling of the aftermath of their lovemaking, Steele held her close as he breathed:

"God, Cassie, you're in my blood! It's as if you were a drug which, continuously injected, soon becomes a deadly habit. Or like a poison that steadily courses through my system, killing me by slow degrees."

Steele kissed her golden brown head, his grip tightening. Then, he said, "Don't ever try and walk out of my life, Cassie. I won't let you! Not ever!" He spoke softly but his words held a thread of harshness and Cassie knew that he meant them.

For a time they lay quietly. Then Steele's arms loosened about her and Cassie knew that his body had relaxed.

Her mind turned to her previous decision to leave Nassau. This man who lay so contentedly by her side had been misjudged by her, unjustly accused. Nowhere in the reports she'd read had she found a single instance of anything other than fairness in his behavior. He had done nothing but good, she realized, nothing but try to rectify Paul's cheating and dishonesty.

And Letty would die for Steele, Cassie thought with compassion for the little woman who seemed to have no world other than that which revolved around "her boy."

She could no longer remain here, Cassie decided, she couldn't be around Steele day after day loving him as she did and having nothing in return but the physical man. She could not stay here as his mistress. Besides, he deserved someone who had more faith in him, would trust him, no matter what.

But she must lay her plans very carefully, she knew, because hadn't Steele told her, only minutes ago, "Don't walk out of my life." So he mustn't know her intentions.

Suddenly the memory of Letty's comments that Steele knew every move Cassie made nudged its way into her thoughts—

"Steele, do you have a private investigator watching me now?" she asked abruptly. "Are you still having me followed, even though Paul hasn't been around?"

"What do you think, little one?" he asked drowsily.

"I don't know. Letty said you were, but I'm asking you."

"Someone is always close by, Cassie, when you are not with me," Steele stated bluntly. "It is for your own good and for my peace of mind. Does it bother you?"

"Yes," she choked.

"Why?"

"I—I just don't like being watched, that's all." Cassie turned in his arms, her large brown eyes searching his face. "Steele, I need my privacy!"

"And you'll have it," he answered promptly.

174

"You mean that you'll call off your watchdog?" she asked hopefully.

"No."

"But, Steele! Why not?"

"It isn't in my best interest to do so." He flicked the tip of her pert nose with his finger. "And I never do anything that isn't in my best interest."

"Then what you're implying is that I'm a prisoner!" Cassie uttered the words in shocked dismay, a tremor in her voice.

"I am implying no such thing," Steele denied calmly. "You are free to go and come as you please. I don't have you locked away in a barred cell, you know. I haven't once fed you bread and water. And I have yet to beat you, although I must say that I have been sorely tempted, on occasion." He chuckled at the look of consternation on Cassie's beautiful young face.

"But, Steele—" she broke off abruptly.

"Yes?" he prompted in his smooth, velvety voice.

"—Uh—never mind!"

"Are you sure?" Steele queried with interest.

"No," Cassie sighed, "I'm really not sure of anything!"

"Well, I am!" he assured her.

Steele's dark head descended and he took Cassie's parted lips with relish, reviving the passion that he knew was always just below the surface. Passion that smoldered, waiting only to be ignited by his touch, then to blaze with a white-hot flame that licked hotly between the two of them.

13

⚶⚶⚶⚶⚶⚶⚶⚶⚶⚶

Cassie brushed the sand from her feet and slipped on the brown, leather-strapped sandals as she made her way up the wide steps of the highrise condominium. She smiled sweetly at the doorman who had greeted her with "Good afternoon, Miss Layton" and a deep bow.

The day was gorgeous, like so many of the beautiful days she had enjoyed in Nassau on this island that she had come to love. Her walks on the beach, no matter what time of the day, always made her feel free and cleared her mind of nagging problems.

But today was special. For all her doubts concerning Steele's involvement in the Paul Malone–Cassie Layton situation had been laid to rest.

Steele had held her in the warm shelter of his arms last night after hours of lovemaking. He had spoken of Paul's and his childhood and of the differences between the two brothers. He had answered all her questions, had held back nothing.

She had been right about the kind of man Steele Malone was, Cassie thought happily, he was just as she had hoped he would be. And although he did have faults— "only small ones," he had stated arrogantly, with his deep, throaty laugh—she knew his strength. A deep, abiding strength.

"It is wonderful what strength of purpose can do," Steele had told her in the wee hours of the night. "It can make a weak man strong, make a strong man gentle, and help one to face uncertainty without flinching."

And when he had asked the question, "What attracted you to me, little one?" Cassie had answered simply, "Your gentleness." Steele had looked at her, his steel-gray eyes questioning and a playful smile tugging at his lips as she had gone on to say, "When I was a little girl, my mother told me, 'Find a man that is strong, dependable and, most of all, a man that is gentle. There's nothing so strong as gentleness, it is the most tender of all feelings and it is love in every way. In every way.'"

Steele had made no reply, had only leaned over to kiss the tip of Cassie's nose. Then, looking down at her, his eyes bright in the dimness of the room, he spoke softly. "It takes an exceptionally uncommon woman to bring out the gentleness that is hidden inside a man, Cassie, and I think I'm entirely correct in saying that you are that extraordinary woman!"

"You certainly use big words, Mr. Malone," she had jested, her fingers playing along his back to tease the flesh and cause Steele's powerful frame to shiver slightly.

"Of course, Miss Layton," he agreed silkily. "That's because I am an uncommon, exceptional, extraordinary man!"

"Not to mention 'conceited,'" Cassie had agreed.

Further conversation had revealed that Steele had not told Paul to lie to her about anything, had not threatened to use Cassie for any reason. She also learned that Steele had gone to the hotel that night to talk to his brother and had seen Paul leave, had heard him give the airport as his destination when he had entered the taxi.

At that point Steele believed that the two must have parted company for good because he had also witnessed the embarrassing scene which had taken place in the casino just prior to Paul's unexpected departure.

Cassie further learned that Steele had threatened his brother's job and security only in a vain attempt to make him stay in Miami with his wife and his child, to assume his responsibility, once and for all, and not go traipsing off on another "great adventure," another sordid affair.

Finally Steele told her that Paul had had no idea that he, Steele, would be in Nassau when he had brought Cassie there, for if he had, Steele felt that the young scalawag would have skipped out sooner than he had.

"He has a silky tongue and a pretty face," the man had said about his younger brother. "But he uses them for all the wrong purposes. He'll end up in a kettle of hot water one of these days and the water will boil and Paul will go under. And I won't be around to pull him out!"

Back to the present, Cassie entered the penthouse to hear the telephone ringing insistently. Deciding that Letty must not be home, Cassie pushed the door closed behind her, ran to the noisy instrument and answered with a breathless, "Hello."

"Now, can you tell me why it is that you can sound so damned seductive at any hour of the day?" the smooth, silky voice of Steele purred from the other end of the line.

Cassie's grip tightened about the receiver. She could almost see the crooked smile form on his sensuous lips, knew that the gray fires were dancing in his eyes as he spoke.

"Hello, Steele." She managed to sound indifferent to his playfulness.

"Hi, honey!" he returned cheerfully. "I suppose Letty's not home or she would have answered the phone."

"I just walked in and the phone was ringing. Letty may be in the laundry room. Shall I check?" she asked hurriedly. Why was it that Steele had such a disturbing effect on her. Though he was only on the telephone and nowhere near her, Cassie felt the blood rush hotly through her veins.

"No," Steele was saying. "That won't be necessary. Just give her a message, if you will. Do you have a pencil handy?"

"A pencil? No, do I need one?" she said somewhat breathlessly. "I mean, is it a long message?"

"Oh, it isn't that it's a long message. It's just that my voice seems to be affecting you in some strange way and I was a bit afraid that you might not remember the message. Or that you might not get it correctly," Steele said huskily, in a deliberately teasing manner.

"I think I'm quite capable of relaying to Letty whatever you wish her to know. This conversation hasn't affected me to any great extent," she lied coolly.

"Okay, honey," he laughed. "Tell Letty that I'm caught in a meeting for the next couple of hours or more, and that she should plan on preparing a late dinner."

"That doesn't sound too difficult, Steele. I believe that I can remember to tell her that."

"Whoa! I'm not finished," he told her. "Also, tell Letty not to go 'all out,' because I have something more important on my mind than eating when I get home!" His meaningful laugh left Cassie shaken.

"I will tell her no such thing!" she shot back.

"Are you telling me that you refuse to give Letty my message?"

"I refuse to give that—that last part, Steele Malone!"

"Uh—oh! Must have touched a raw nerve, she's

179

calling me 'Steele Malone,' " he spoke as if to himself. Then came his deep chuckle along the wire and he continued silkily, "Can I help it if I miss you, Cassie? After all, I'm not made of stone, you know. In fact, I'm a sinfully human man!"

"Steele, I think I hear Letty at the door. Would you like to wait and talk to her?" Cassie was well aware that the woman was nowhere around but the conversation was getting somewhat out of hand.

"No, just tell her I called. Oh, one other thing, Cassie. Paul has gone back to Miami so don't worry about running into him. See you tonight, honey." And he hung up.

Cassie stood staring down at the receiver in her hand for a moment before replacing it in its cradle. Steele had used the endearment, "honey," three times, she had counted them. He had said it as naturally as anyone would who was accustomed to using the endearment to a loved one. Steele had told her that he missed her, had spoken with his customary honesty.

She felt her resolve weakening, her decision to leave Steele about to dissolve. He was a master with words and, not even knowing her intention to leave, had skillfully undermined her determination to go.

Shaking her head, Cassie felt suddenly as if she were about to be drawn into Steele's web. Like the spider and the fly, she thought feebly. The spider weaves its trap, spinning its fine web, then sits back easily and contentedly to await his prey. In his arrogance, he is confident that the fly will soon willingly enter the waiting lure. And the fly does just that. It wings into the silky, lacy net where it is hopelessly captured, with no possible escape.

This was exactly where Cassie saw herself. She had been lured toward that silken web and she was now so near that she could feel the tendrils teasing her flesh, enticing her, tempting her to draw even closer, attracting her with the promise of gained pleasure and reward. The pleasure of Steele's passion. The reward of perhaps one day having his love.

But it was only a decoy, Cassie was wise enough to realize, an attractive appeal used to catch unsuspecting prey. For, once captured, it could mean only certain defeat, and all but the trusting fly were aware that the spider waited for the satisfaction of devouring its innocent victim.

Sighing heavily, Cassie headed up the stairs. This was the time, it was now, or never! She would pack her bags and leave Nassau, she determined, leave while Steele was attending his meeting and while Letty was out. And Paul had left, she remembered Steele telling her. That was the only thing Cassie could honestly feel good about.

Reaching for the seat belt, Cassie buckled it about her small waist, then leaned back against the soft, cushioned head rest. She closed her eyes and, with a breath of relief, listened to the roar of engines and the rustle as other passengers moved about the plane and settled into their seats.

"Please!" she whispered urgently. "Please, plane, hurry and get off the ground!"

She had watched over her shoulder all the way to the airport, imploring the taxi driver to hurry so she would get to the airport before Steele had time to learn where she had gone. She had seen the small black car pull out from the curb and fall in line a few cars behind the taxi as it left the condominium.

Cassie remembered her uneasiness as she stood in line for her ticket. She had watched the man in jeans, T-shirt, and dark glasses as he had followed at a distance as she moved down the corridor. And he stood at the row of pay phones while she checked in at the departure gate.

She knew this was the man Steele had hired to follow

her and that it was Steele whom the man was calling but felt hopeful that he could not be reached since she knew that he was in a meeting.

Cassie had glanced repeatedly at her small watch as the hands seemed to drag from one slow minute to the next. When she wasn't looking at the watch she had been searching the crowd for Steele's dark head. She had been, and still was, a nervous wreck.

At one point Cassie thought the man might try and stop her, prevent her from boarding the plane. Then she reminded herself that he couldn't apprehend her. He was a private investigator, not a policeman, and besides, she had done no wrong! But she had been somewhat surprised that the man had not purchased a ticket and followed her on the plane.

Even now, buckled into her seat, Cassie couldn't completely relax until the plane was airborne because she knew Steele Malone well. She had no doubt that he would board the plane and arrogantly drag her off. She shivered at the thought.

The roar of the engines lessened to a hum and the plane moved slightly. The high-pitched chime sounded, bringing her attention to the Fasten Seat Belt and No Smoking signs which lit up overhead, and Cassie's heart beat faster. The plane began a snail's-pace progress, away from the terminal and toward the runway.

Cassie had not realized the deathlike grip with which she held on to both arms of her seat until a voice beside her spoke solicitously. "Don't be afraid, dear. Is this your first flight?"

Cassie turned to the older woman seated next to her. The woman smiled as her light blue eyes glanced at Cassie's hands and back to her face. Then Cassie's own gaze traveled to her hands and she saw that her grip was so tight that her knuckles were white. She was so tense that she felt like a fine china doll and that if she moved, she would break.

"No—no, I'm not afraid of flying," she managed to assure the woman, but the lady only smiled and covered Cassie's hand with her own momentarily, then patted it, saying, "You'll be all right once we're in the air, my dear."

"Yes. Yes, I'm sure I will—very sure!" Cassie returned, moving her hands to fold them into her lap. How right the lady was, she thought grimly, how right!

It seemed that no sooner had the stewardess welcomed them aboard Flight 86 bound for Miami and points north than she was announcing their approach to the Miami airport and that she hoped they had enjoyed their flight and would fly with them again.

As the plane nosed into its assigned stopping place, Cassie stood and waited none too patiently for an opening into the aisle into which the passengers had converged. She could hardly wait to get her luggage and escape from the airport. She had decided to call Susie and ask if the girl would let her stay there for a few days until she could make other arrangements.

Walking down the long concourse, Cassie moved with the flow of humanity, her mind filled with her thoughts, wondering what she would do if she couldn't reach Susie. She missed Letty already and, in spite of herself, she missed Steele and wished briefly that he *had* reached the Nassau airport before she left. Her fanciful mind visualized him showing up at the last minute, declaring undying love and dragging her off the plane.

Cassie laughed shakily at her fantasy as she stepped onto the escalator to ride the mobile stairway downward to the baggage claim area. She waited with her fellow passengers while the various sizes and colors of luggage slid onto the baggage dispenser and each passenger claimed his own.

Finally after what seemed hours to the impatient girl, Cassie's own luggage appeared and she retrieved it and made her way to the gate, handing her ticket to the attendant. He seemed to take his time in assuring himself that the stubs matched before allowing her through the gate.

Cassie again rode the mechanical stairs; this time she rode upward to the street level of the terminal.

"Cassie!"

She heard her name thundered out and her heart stood still for a split second before it began to beat like a trip-hammer, pounding against her rib cage with such force she could hardly breathe.

Looking downward over her shoulder Cassie's searching eyes rested upon the broad shoulders and dark head which towered inches above the pushing, shoving crowd which thronged the baggage area below. Steele Malone was making his way through the crowd toward the escalator.

Cassie was only halfway up and when she saw Steele step onto the bottom step of the moving stairs she began to climb, frantically pushing her way past startled people. Another glance showed her that Steele was doing the same, taking two steps at a time.

"Cassie!" Steele's voice carried above the rumble of voices and the noises of the busy terminal.

Suddenly Cassie was seized by iron-hard hands and the loud roar of jet engines drowned out the heartrending scream which escaped her lips. She turned to look into the smoky-gray eyes of Steele Malone.

"Where the hell do you think you're going?" he demanded angrily.

"Away! As far away from you as I can go!" Cassie shouted savagely and almost fell as the escalator reached its destination.

Steele's strong arm steadied her and he ushered her

away from the flow of human traffic. Conscious of the curious stares coming their way, Cassie tried to pull free of his grip. She felt utterly defeated. She had spent the last of her money, the money she had once offered Steele, on taxi fare and a plane ticket and had endured agonizing moments as she had fled Nassau.

All to no avail! Steele had prevailed, he had won and Cassie had lost! It was Steele's triumph, his victory, and Cassie's attempt at freedom had been thwarted. She had failed miserably.

"I won't let you do this to me, Cassie!" he rasped furiously. "I won't stand for it!"

In her struggle to free herself from Steele's grip, Cassie dropped her luggage. As he bent to pick up the fallen bags, Cassie made to run but Steele was quicker than she. Again she felt that relentless grip on her arms.

Steele spun her around and crushed her to him, unleashing all the longings and desires hidden deep within Cassie's being. She had tried to make herself believe that she could get over Steele once she was away from him.

But with his rock-hard leanness pressed against her soft flesh and his lips only a fleeting breath away, Cassie struggled to control her urgent need to surrender. She was sorely tempted to give in, to lean against the warmth of Steele, to belong to him, to be with him no matter what the circumstances.

"Did you really believe I'd just let you walk out of my life?" Steele asked in a ragged, uneven voice. "I warned you, Cassie. I warned you that you were never to try to walk out of my life."

Steele shook Cassie vigorously before he admitted chokingly, "God! I saw the danger signs the night I first laid eyes on you! Dear God!" he groaned feelingly. "Why didn't I make you leave while I still could? Christ!"

"Then why didn't you? Why didn't you send me

away?" Cassie flared at him unreasonably. Unshed tears were stinging and burning her eyelids.

"Because—" Steele began huskily. "Because love is more powerful than reason, little one!"

"Love?" Cassie stared wide-eyed at the man who towered above her.

"Yes, Cassie, love! And it's as frustrating as hell!" Steele admitted sheepishly. As she stood gaping at him in astonishment, his laughter rang out happily. "I wanted you before I ever even knew you. And then when I met you—there was something there from the beginning. A dangerous, magnetic attraction that seemed ever-present. It was so strong that it frightened me, yet it was something I wanted, needed, and had to have!"

"What about Helen? You had her!" Cassie flung at him. She felt that she had to know how Steele felt about the other woman.

"I never touched Helen once after I met you!" he stated firmly. "I didn't want her, and I hadn't wanted her in a very long time. I slept on that damned sofa in the library, when I *did* sleep. I spent wakeful, restless hours fighting the impelling urge to climb those stairs and take you—to make love to you—to make you mine!

"My God, Cassie! You left me soulless from wanting you! I had actually fallen in love with you, although I wouldn't admit it, not even to myself. And you were in love with my worthless brother! It damned near drove me insane! I loved you, Cassie. God, how I loved you!"

"And *now,* Steele?" Cassie whispered hopefully, her warm breath mingling with his as she looked up at him, her soul in her eyes. "What about *now?*"

"Oh, Cassie, Cassie! Need you even ask?" Steele sighed heavily as he gathered her closer into his embrace. "I love you more than life itself, my darling. I can't even imagine life without you, without loving you, without having your love!"

"And I do love you!" she cried happily. "I love you! I never knew what love really was until I met you!"

"Then you'll come back home with me, be my lover, my friend, and my wife?" Steele whispered, his eyes a deep, smoky gray.

And Cassie answered with a whispered "Yes! Oh, yes!"

Then Steele's lips took Cassie's with sweet, tender possessiveness. And with the certain knowledge that she knew that he belonged to her as she belonged to him.

Silhouette Desire
15-Day Trial Offer

A new romance series that explores contemporary relationships in exciting detail

Four Silhouette Desire romances, free for 15 days!
We'll send you four new Silhouette Desire romances to look over for 15 days, absolutely free! If you decid not to keep the books, return them and owe nothing.

Four books a month, free home delivery. If you like Silhouette Desire romances as much as we think you will, keep them and return your payment with the invoice. Then we will send you four new books every month to preview, just as soon as they are published. You pay only for the books you decide to keep, and you never pay postage and handling.

Silhouette Desire

Coming Next Month

Velvet Touch by Stephanie James

Tawny, elegant Lacey Sheldon was determined to
cut loose from her librarian's past and find
liberation out west. This island paradise in Puget
Sound seemed the perfect place to begin . . . until
she met Holt Randolph. He said he didn't want
half a heart, and challenged her to gamble it
all in a blazing affair that would bring
her to her senses—and into his arms.

The Cowboy And The Lady by Diana Palmer

Jace had given Amanda her first taste of passion.
His silver eyes had held a forbidden fascination for
her, but at sixteen she'd been too inexperienced to
understand the fiery message in his searing kisses.
Now Amanda was ready to learn the lessons of
desire, and there was only one man who could
teach her—a man whose glittering gaze held
the secrets of her unhappy past and the
promise of a golden future.

Silhouette Desire

Coming Next Month

Come Back, My Love by Pamela Wallace

TV newsperson Toni Lawrence was on the fast track to fame when photographer Theo Chakaris swept her off her feet at the Royal Wedding. How had she abandoned herself to this adventurer? Storybook romances belonged to princes and princesses. She tried to forget, to bury herself in her work, but passion brought them together to recapture the glory of ecstasy.

Blanket Of Stars by Lorraine Valley

Greece was the perfect setting for adventure and romance. But for Glena Fielding it became more. This land she would call home. In Alex Andreas' dark eyes she saw a passion and a glory, a flame to light her senses and melt her resistance beneath the searing Greek sun. In his arms she became invincible as he led her to the stars.